COLORFUL, DESCRIPTIVE, FASCINATINGLY PROVOCATIVE... Andrea Hurtt's *Masquerade*, is a *WONDERFUL* story about relationships and consequences. Just when you think you know what happens next, you realize *THAT YOU DON'T!* Not by a long shot, because that's what deception is... a mind trick that lets you think you've got it all figured out. At least until everything unravels. This is a *FANTASTIC* first novel and I can't wait to see what stories Andrea Hurtt weaves next.

Deb White- *Staff Writer for Nerds and Beyond*

From the moment I opened *Nebraska Nights*, I couldn't put it down! I immediately connected with the characters, experiencing the *EMOTIONS* and *TENSION* as I turned each page. Enraptured in their lives, I wanted more! If you love a *SPICY, RIVETING, PAGE TURNER*, you will fall in love with every encounter, leaving you wanting more; more hunting, more passion, and more *Gene, Tom, Jessica, and Alex*!

Kimberly Raff - *Executive Director at* **Foster Alumni Mentors**

DEPOT DREAMS

BOOK TWO

DEMONS WITH US SERIES

ANDREA HURTT

LINDA STECKER

PIECE OF PIE PUBLISHING

Piece Of Pie Publishing

11923 NE Sumner ST Ste 826515

Portland, OR 97220-9601"

PROLOGUE

"Am I dead?" Lacey asked.

"I am sorry, love," the dark figure said.

The woman dressed in black towered over her; she must've been at least five feet nine inches tall. Her hair was long, curly, and the perfect blend of black and brown that complimented her mocha skin. She should've given off a sense of intimidation or even fear.

However, she felt no fear standing next to her.

Finally breaking her eyes away from the dark figure, Lacey looked at the scene before her.

They were in an old building, a factory of some sort that clearly hadn't been in use for many years. The large room was empty except for the four people shackled to concrete pillars.

She sighed at the sight of her lifeless body chained to the closest pillar and sitting on the floor. A slight smile curved her lips, but her appearance resembled someone who'd been abandoned in the desert to perish.

Her skin was gray and wrinkled, devoid of any moisture or

shine of health. There was nothing left of her but skin and bones. She didn't look her age, twenty-four.

She dared look at the other three. An old man who was dressed as if he were homeless, a teenage girl, and a man in a jogging suit too big for his frame.

They all looked emaciated and wrinkled, but alive.

Lacey turned to the woman beside her. "What's happening? The last thing I knew, I was lying on a beach in Costa Rica with a margarita in my hand. And now…"

"The creature that ended your life put you in the perfect dream world, but it was only a dream. Your time has come. We need to go."

She glanced at the tall woman in black. "Creature? What— And go where? I don't look like I'm in any shape to go anywhere."

The woman smiled, filling her with warmth, like the love of a mother.

"You have done all you can here, but you must leave this plane of existence. Now you can rest."

"What about the others? We can't leave them here to dry out, like me. We gotta do something!"

"Fear not, Lacey. They will finish out their lives the way it is ordained. Someone will be along soon to help." The figure put her hand on the Lacey's shoulder and repeated herself. "It's time."

"But… I don't even know your name," Lacey said.

"I am simply known as a reaper. Please, take my hand."

She obeyed and looked back at her deceased body one last time before fading away.

Alex sat up in bed. It was just a dream, a bizarre dream, but just a dream. She flopped back on her pillow and tried to go back to sleep.

CHAPTER ONE

Gene

"Missing Arvada, Colorado teen has found. All hope had been lost that seventeen-year-old Conner Stewart would ever be found," the news anchor announced on the TV. "The teen went missing a few months ago, with several others. Six of the teenagers had been found at an abandoned sanatorium but with no trace of Conner. The others had all acknowledged he'd been with them when they'd entered the building, but they'd been separated and lost track of him once inside. A thorough search had been conducted of the building and the surrounding lands, still with no trace. It's been two months, and Conner has now turned up, unharmed, in Philadelphia, Pennsylvania. The teen claims he has no memory of how he ended up over sixteen hundred miles from home but authorities…"

Gene shut off the television. Closure like this was rarely achieved.

He and Tom had both felt bad leaving Colorado without

finding the kid, but had marked it off as unlikely they'd ever find him. They released the ghosts in the sanatorium and moved on.

Gene didn't bother trying to guess what'd happened to the kid. He was alive. That was all that mattered unless, of course, they heard of strange happenings in Philadelphia and had to go check it out. He should have Tom check it out when he got back to the depot.

He made his way to the kitchen and grabbed a beer out of the refrigerator. Leaning against the counter, he popped open the bottle and looked around at the place he'd called home for the last three years.

It was an old, abandoned train depot, out in the middle of nowhere. Esbon, Kansas had a population of sixty-seven people— sixty-nine if anyone knew about the two men that'd taken up residence in the old building.

It was a one-story brick building with a full, finished basement. The exterior had fallen into disrepair and the windows were all boarded up.

When Gene's father had found it, he'd just intended to camp there for the night between jobs. He'd soon discovered there was a basement tornado shelter, but it'd been converted to living quarters for the train personnel.

The place was centrally located for hunting across the country, and, for some reason, the electricity had never been shut off after the depot had been abandoned for more modern modes of transportation.

The stairs from the back room of the depot led down the outside wall into a large, open rectangular room. To the right of the staircase was a long wooden table with seating for six.

The room was open to a recreation room with sparse furniture. Behind the recreation room were four bedrooms lined down the hallway. On the opposite side of the hall was the kitchen and a large bathroom that was more like one in an RV park than something in a home. Beyond that, there were two more bedrooms.

There were no windows in the basement, which worked to

their advantage because no one could see in when the lights were on.

They'd done some cleaning in the main rooms, but it was a bachelor pad, and they weren't there very often. They had some non-perishable foods in the kitchen and weapons of every variety tucked into an extra bedroom.

The large wooden table was supposed to be for dining, but it held stacks of books, and newspaper articles of the things they hunted.

There were even old children's books. They'd collected anything on their travels that helped them with the mythology and lore of the things that most people would never believe were real.

Gene's dad believed even fairytales could hold real history in them and he'd taught him not to overlook information just because it came from a non-traditional source.

He and his cousin, Tom, had added to the furnishings, including a big-screen television. They'd smuggled in some furniture under the cover of darkness to make it feel like a home, but transporting furniture in the Mustang was hard.

They parked the vintage car on the loading platform on the track side of the depot, away from the town, where it wouldn't be seen and would be covered from the weather.

Gene heard the rumble of the engine. He grabbed another beer.

Tom was back. He made his way downstairs into the rec room and set the two brown paper bags on the table before pulling out a chair.

Gene set the bottle in front of his cousin.

The table could seat eight people with room to spare. Yet, they always sat in the same seats on the far-left side.

There was a small cafe in town they grabbed food from, and even ate inside once in a while. Jimmy's Café had the best burgers Gene had ever tasted—and he'd had burgers from coast to coast.

He could eat one every day. Unfortunately, his cousin had

pointed out they didn't want to be seen there too often, or people might notice they were 'local'.

As far as the café people knew, they were business executives passing through, just for the sake of a really good burger. So far, they believed it.

Gene took a big breath and tried to be subtle about it. It was good that Tom was back. If he had someone to talk to, then he wouldn't be thinking about *her*.

It'd been a couple of months now, and despite the passing of time, he hadn't been able to wipe her from his mind. Even when he was busy hunting, he still dreamed of her at night, running his fingers through her thick dark hair and feeling the curves of her body pressed to his. His body responded just thinking about her.

What was it about her that had him so enraptured?

He'd been with lots of women, but none of them had affected him like this.

Gene's stomach clenched every time he thought about the day he'd left.

It was his biggest regret.

**Jessica*

Fourteen weeks.

The exact amount of days only involved a quick count, but Jessica didn't want to think about that detail. It hurt to think about how long it'd been since he'd left, taking his cousin with him.

She'd been so hurt that he hadn't said goodbye. She'd waited for a call, a text, anything to let her know he was still thinking about her.

Nothing ever came.

Slowly, she'd moved on.

Jessica had traded in her old, beat-up van for something more economical. Her new red Ford Focus was a lot more comfortable for the long rides back and forth to the closest town, Broken Bow, Nebraska.

She'd gotten back into sewing her custom quilts for her online business. Unfortunately, that had left her with lots of time to think as she watched the material fly through her hands and the needle of the sewing machine moved up and down in quick succession.

Her mind always drifted to thoughts of Gene.

Jessica sat in the driver's seat, her car parked in front of the farmhouse. Her hands still gripped the steering wheel as she stared at her home.

The old three-story farmhouse had a wrap-around porch, with steps that lead up to the door in the center of the first floor, with large windows on either side.

The second floor had four windows across, and on the third floor was the attic that was split in two, with an oval window on the right side, and a standard rectangular window on the left.

The farmstead had been passed down for four generations, always to the eldest daughter, as tradition. Her great Aunt Marge had been the last owner. She'd never married, but her younger sister had. So, the house would have passed to Marge's niece, Jessica's mother. Her mom, Jenifer, hadn't wanted it. She'd offered it to Jessica, who now lived in the home with her best friend, Alex, and the ghost of her Great-Great-Great-Grandmother, Judith.

She tried not to think about the ghost.

She wasn't afraid, but Alex was.

Not to mention, thinking of Judith also brought up memories of the guys.

Gene and Tom stayed at the house in order to get rid of the ghost for them, but before that could happen, they'd found a Wendigo living down by the lake, and that had been much more dangerous.

They'd killed the monster and saved the victims that were still alive.

Then they left.

Alex had taken a shine to fixing up the farm. She'd started

with the house, cleaning every nook and cranny, fixing things she had the skill for.

Anything to keep her hands and her mind busy. They'd taken the time to power wash the wood slates of the old place and applied a fresh coat of white paint.

To the right of the house was the large red barn. Alex had two horses that still refused to go inside, even after living there for over two months.

Jessica understood what that felt like. She didn't want to go inside as if staying in the car would make things not reality. However, sitting in the car wouldn't undo what was done.

What was she going to do? The news she held could be the best thing that ever happened to her or the hardest.

Possibly a bit of both.

Jessica sighed and got out of her car. She couldn't see what the future held, but she'd have to face it, no matter what came.

CHAPTER
TWO

CHAPTER TWO

Alex

Alex trotted down the stairs. There was noise in the kitchen, so Jessica was back. She'd just finished clearing a clog in the bathtub upstairs. She headed to the small breakfast table, pulling out one of the two wire-wound-backed chairs. The small round table looked like it belonged in a 1950s soda shop more than their kitchen, but it was cute. She cocked her head as her friend opened and closed every cupboard before pulling leftovers out of the fridge.

Jessica still didn't say anything, even though there was no way she didn't know Alex had joined her.

"Well, what did the doctor say?" Alex prompted.

"I'm fine," Jessica said, her voice hard.

"No, you're not fine. You can't keep anything down, and you haven't been sleeping. Something's going on," she retorted. "You can't keep pretending nothing is wrong."

Her bestie caught her eye, her expression unreadable. "I guess there's no point in drawing this out." She let out a long sigh. "Yes, something's wrong. But not what you think. What's *wrong* is the fact they aren't coming back."

"Jess, you've got to let this go. I can't believe you're still hung up—"

"I'm pregnant," she barked, dropping into the seat across from Alex.

She blinked and shook her head. "Pregnant? How do you feel about that?" She was cautious because she couldn't guess from her best friend's guarded demeanor how she should react. She would be there for Jessica, no matter how she felt, or what she wanted to do, of course.

"I don't know. On the one hand, I'm excited. I mean, can you imagine how cute this kid is going to be with Gene as his dad? But, I'm also scared…because what kinda mom am I going to be?"

"You're gonna be a great mom. I'll be here to help you," Alex said. She waited for a moment before asking the inevitable question. "Are you going to tell Gene?"

Jessica dropped her face into her hands. "I don't know."

"He has a right to know," she whispered.

"Does he? He left without even saying goodbye after telling me I was everything he ever wanted. Not to mention, the most amazing sex I've ever had. Don't guys usually come back for more if it's that good?"

"They got a call and had to go."

"You've said that before, but it still doesn't seem right to me. How could he get a call for a new job, pack up, make Tom pack, and leave, all before I even got out of the shower? Hell, he could've interrupted my shower. I haven't heard from him since he left. It's like he completely forgot about me." Jessica let out another defeated sigh. "Besides, you know what his life is like."

"Have you tried to contact him?"

"What?" Jessica asked, her eyes wide.

"Well, I didn't hear from Tom for over a week, so I texted him and we've been chatting ever since. They aren't used to having someone who cares about them."

"You've been talking to Tom, and you didn't tell me before now?" Jessica frowned. "Does he mention Gene?"

"Occasionally, but mostly we just talk about his cases and the repairs to the farm."

Jessica looked down, and her mouth quivered.

"You should call him. Ask him to come see you. Then tell him when he's here."

"I don't know. I don't think I can deal with him popping in and out of my kid's life. He'll breeze into town and get me all riled up and then leave. I'll never have a normal relationship again," her friend all but moaned.

"Or you'll be angry all the time because you never see him," Alex said.

"But what will I tell my kid? 'Sorry, honey. Daddy can't come to your game. He's trying to kill a Wendigo.' Would it be fair to them?" Now Jessica was exasperated. She tossed her hands up. "I've already mentally had this argument with myself on the drive home and haven't come to any conclusions."

"Maybe he'll stay," Alex said, hopefully.

"I seriously doubt it. He couldn't wait to get out of here." Tears filled Jessica's aquamarine eyes.

"Oh, I think you're blowing that out of proportion. They had trouble and had to go. Even Tom seemed worried. And you never know. If he had a reason to stay..."

"Maybe..." Jessica said.

"Keep in mind, the psychic at that birthday party years ago said he was your soulmate," she teased.

"Yeah, right!" Jessica glared.

———

Weeks went by. Thanksgiving was looming, just a few days away, and Jessica still hadn't decided whether or not to tell Gene. Alex was at her wit's end and wasn't afraid to voice her opinion.

She hated lying to Tom. They talked occasionally but mostly texted. She tried to keep him talking about hunting, telling him her life was the same boring thing day after day. Still, was he getting suspicious of her avoiding talking about Jessica? Had he noticed she hadn't mentioned her bestie much?

"So, what do you want for dinner?" Alex asked.

"A big greasy burger," Jessica said.

She laughed.

Her best friend was in her second trimester and her morning sickness had finally subsided; she was getting her appetite back. Thanks to her long torso, she was barely showing, although she was almost four months along.

"I don't think we have any ground beef in the freezer. Do you want to go to the tavern and have one?" Alex asked.

"Yes! And onion rings!"

"Well, I need to get cleaned up first," Alex said, brushing the hay off her shirt. Their neighbor, Beau, lived a few miles down the road and had been helping her bale hay.

She'd spent the day loading the bales in her truck with his help, then had hauled them back to the barn to store them for winter. She refused to let Jessica help and put any strain on the baby.

It didn't take Alex long to shower and slip into a dress, and they headed to the tavern.

As they looked over the menu, Alex played with the necklace that Tom had given her. It was a silver unicursal hexagram with a circle of flames around it, the same as his tattoo.

She always wore it, not only because it was for protection, but because it made her feel close to him.

They ate and discussed the preparations they needed to make for their first winter on the farm. When they were almost finished eating, their server came back to their table.

"Are you the ones who do that dance?" she asked.

The girl was referring to a line dance they'd done with the guys a couple of months back.

"Yeah, the sleazy slide," Jessica said.

"Would you teach it to me?" the waitress asked.

Jessica glanced at Alex.

"You're the teacher. Go teach her." Alex smirked.

"You gotta come, too."

"I'm not done eating. You teach her the steps and I'll come dance with you in a minute."

"All right," Jessica said.

Alex watched her teach the girl the line dance.

When they played *You Shook Me All Night Long*, Alex finally went and joined them. Her legs were already tired from hauling hay, so by the end of the dance, she felt like Jello and was ready to go home.

Jessica was still talking to the server, so Alex went outside for some fresh air, despite the fact it was quite cold, even for November.

"That was some dance." A lanky man stepped outside and lit up a cigarette. He was short and scruffy, wearing a dirty cowboy hat soaked with sweat stains.

Alex ignored him, resting against the wall of the building, trying to ignore the speeding up of her heart.

He came over, planting a hand next to her on the wall, leaning into her.

He smelled of beer and cigarettes, causing her nose to burn.

"I'd like to show you some of my moves," he slurred before trying to move in to kiss her.

Alex dipped and sidestepped.

The guy fell into the wall face-first. Blood spurted from his nose from the impact, and he covered his face with both hands.

She tried to duck back inside to avoid him, but he grabbed her arm with a bloody hand.

"Let go of me before you really regret it," Alex spat, reaching for her necklace without a thought.

His eyes flicked to the charm around her neck. "What's that? The devil's symbol? Are you a witch or something?"

She wrenched her arm away and glared, muttering under her breath. She stormed back inside to find Jessica.

Her best friend was dancing with a shaggy-haired man.

Jessica stopped dead in her tracks when she saw her friend. "Alex, what happened?"

"We need to go," she said through gritted teeth.

The guy she'd encountered outside burst through the door behind Alex. Blood ran down his face, and he threw her a dark look before dashing for the bathroom.

"What the hell is going on here?" the shaggy-haired man Jessica had been dancing with demanded.

Alex ignored him. "We're leaving."

"Like hell you are," the man grabbed Alex. "You're sticking 'round till the cops get here. You assaulted my friend."

Alex struggled to get free, but he had a solid grip on her arm. The more she pulled to get away, the tighter his grip became.

"Let go of her," Jessica ordered, trying to step between Alex and the man.

"No, Pete, call the sheriff."

"I said, let go!" Jessica said, her voice raised, as she tried to remove the man's hand off Alex.

He shoved her aside, knocking her into a table.

The round wooden bar table broke with a loud creak from the impact.

"Jess!" Alex yelled, fearing for her bestie's unborn child.

"Whoa! What's all this about?" the big burly bartender demanded, darting to help Jessica up.

Alex pulled from the hold again, anger and panic stirring in her gut. Jessica's baby!

"He won't let go of my friend and he just shoved me," her best friend shouted.

"Bill, you wanna explain this?" the bartender asked.

"You better ask Jack. He went outside to make sure this lady was all right, and he came back with a bloody nose."

"So that gives you the right to shove her friend down?" the bartender growled.

"What seems to be the trouble here?"

Sheriff Wilson asked, striding toward them. He was a stout old man, a full gray beard, light blue eyes, and past retirement age.

Everyone started talking at once, everyone except Alex.

"Whoa, whoa, whoa!" the sheriff barked, holding up his hands. "First off, Bill, turn her loose." He pointed to the grip on Alex's arm.

"I's just tryin' to keep her from boltin'," Bill said, but he obeyed.

Her arm had a red mark that would end up being a bruise; his grip had been that tight.

"Why would she bolt?" the sheriff asked.

"'Cause she assaulted Jack," Bill said.

"Where is Jack? He can speak for himself," the sheriff said.

"He's in the bathroom with a bloody nose."

"Well then, I think I'll escort this lady outside and get her side of the story, then I'll talk to Jack. Meantime, you stay put," he said, pointing to Bill. He turned to Alex and gestured to the door.

Alex frowned and cast a frightened glance at Jessica. She didn't want to talk to the lawman, but she didn't want to go to jail, either. Outside, she told the sheriff what had happened.

"And then he grabbed you?" Sheriff Wilson asked, his gaze on the bloody handprint on her arm and the splatter on her dress.

"Yes. I swear I didn't touch him. I was just trying to get away." Tears were sliding down her cheeks. She wanted Tom.

"I believe you, honey," he said in a reassuring, fatherly voice. "Those boys like to get into all kinds of trouble when they've had a few too many. But I think it's best you head home and not go back in. Do you need anything from in there?"

"Just my friend, Jessica. She has the car keys."

"All right, you wait here. I'll go collect her and get you on your way, then I'll straighten those boys out. Don't you worry. They shouldn't bother ya'll again."

"Thank you, Sheriff."

CHAPTER THREE

Alex

Back at home, Alex took her necklace off and hung it on the hook by the mirror. She slipped into the steaming bathtub with a sigh. She was exhausted—now mentally, as well as physically.

She'd told Jessica what'd happened on the way home, and by the time they reached the house, she was shaking.

"I wish I could do something for you, like fixing you a drink, but we don't have any alcohol in the house. I appreciate you going dry with me since I can't drink," her best friend gingerly touched her tiny pooch of a belly. "But you could really use something tonight."

Alex had settled for aromatherapy bath salts and Tylenol PM to help her relax.

She looked up at the necklace.

"A devil's symbol, indeed." Actually, it was quite the opposite. She'd done a little research about the symbol after Tom had given it to her.

The name *unicursal hexagram* came from the fact that it could be drawn unicursally—or in one continuous line instead of two separate triangles. It also has the name of the *Guardian Spirit*.

She lay in the warm water, wishing Tom was there. None of this would've happened if he'd been here. She wished she could call him and ask him to come visit, but if Tom came, so would Gene, and Jessica still hadn't told Gene about the baby.

Alex contemplated calling Tom anyway, to force Jessica to tell Gene, but she couldn't do that to her friend. Jessica would never do that to her.

She just wanted to be with Tom.

Alex stayed in the bathtub until the water went cold and her skin was as wrinkled as prunes. Sleepily, she dressed in her pajamas and went to bed.

She woke up during the night, and her bladder ached with fullness. She stepped over the meticulous salt circle that Tom had placed around her bed.

She'd wanted to sweep it up several times. They hadn't heard a peep out of Grams since they'd killed the Wendigo. However, every time she grabbed the broom, Alex remembered Tom placing the salt there to protect her. She'd become accustomed to stepping over it.

A chill shot down her spine when she went back to her room a few minutes later. Alex froze in the doorframe. "Judith?" she asked quietly. "Um, Grams? Damn," she said to the empty room. "I have no idea what to call this ghost."

The feeling of warm comfort floated over her and the nickname *Grams* floated in her head.

"All right, Grams it is."

Alex stepped further into the room, intending to return to her warm bed. There was a rush of wind toward her, lifting the edge of her pajama shirt, and mussing her hair. A second chill went up her spine, covering her skin with goose flesh. Suddenly, Alex wasn't in control of her own body anymore.

· · ·

Judith

Something was wrong, and Judith simply could not stand by and watch. The red moon had risen, and trouble was coming. She had to get Edith to safety. She couldn't let her daughter get hurt, even if she was pregnant out of wedlock.

She floated into Jessica's room, placed her hands on the younger woman's shoulders, and shook her hard to wake her.

"We have to go," Judith urged.

"Alex? What the hell are you doing?" Jessica snapped, her tone equal parts irritated and sleepy. "Go back to bed."

"Get up, now! Trouble is coming, we need to go!" she repeated, pulling the covers off Jessica.

Well, no wonder she got herself in the family way; her night clothes barely covered the essentials. If I had been around to raise her, I would never have let her dress like this. The thoughts ran through her mind, wrapped in disapproval.

Judith wrangled a sleepy Jessica downstairs and grabbed a jacket off the coat rack, handing it to the dark-haired girl as they made their way outside. She closed the front door and headed straight for the barn.

"Alex, where are we going?" Jessica asked when they walked past the large, empty horse stalls, continuing back further into the dark barn.

"Shh! We need to be quiet," Judith ordered, moving deeper into the building. She stopped at the back of the barn and used her whole body to push a heavy shelving unit back. The ground was uneven, so it tipped over with a tremendous clatter.

"So much for being quiet," Jessica said sarcastically.

"Hush up!" Judith lifted a heavy wooden door that was practically hidden on the floor of the barn. Dirt and hay had obscured it.

"What the hell?" Jessica exclaimed. "I had absolutely no clue there was a door there. How did you know? You never mentioned it before."

"Come on! Go down inside. And watch your mouth or I'll wash it out with soap." She waved her into the dark hole.

"Alex, I don't—"

"Edith, get your rear down there before I turn you over my knee," Judith said, grabbing the sleeve of the girl's jacket and pulling her in the dark but safe place. "Go to the bottom of the ramp and turn left."

"Edith? What-"

Judith put a hand on Jessica's lower back and gave her a gentle push to get her moving down the ramp and stopped.

"Alex, we need a light," Jessica said.

"Keep going!" Judith said.

The girl obeyed, holding onto the wall as she went.

Judith watched until her daughter disappeared from view into the darkness.

Judith let the door drop into place and grabbed the handle to bolt it.

The iron handle sent Alex flying backward as it ejected Judith from inside her.

Alex's head hit the top of the door frame, knocking her unconscious. She toppled to the floor and rolled off the right side of the ramp.

Gene

Gene drove on. It was the middle of the night, and he focused on the dark road ahead of him. They'd just finished a job in McAllen, Texas, and they were on their way back to Kansas.

His sleeping cousin sat bolt upright in his seat. "We gotta go back!" Tom yelled.

"We *are* headed back.".

"Not to the depot. We need to go to Nebraska. The girls are in danger," Tom said, leaning forward in his seat to look out the windshield.

"How do you know that?" Gene asked. He frowned and leaned forward, too, catching sight of the red moon his cousin was staring at. Nothing good had ever happened when they'd seen a red moon.

"Just trust me, and step on it!" Tom said, exasperation lacing his voice.

He floored it, heading for Broken Bow. He wanted to argue, but he trusted Tom's gut as much as his own. So, if Tom said something was wrong, something was wrong.

Somehow, Tom and Alex had an unexplained bond. Did it have something to do with her healing him when the Wendigo almost killed him? Maybe it had connected them somehow.

Tom had tried to explain it, but Gene had struggled to wrap his mind around it.

However, since they'd been on the road, he'd noted several times that Tom grabbed his phone *before* it rang when Alex was calling. Sometimes Tom paused in the middle of something, like he was seeing something else, and when he'd come back, Gene asked about it.

He'd simply say Alex wasn't feeling well, and he needed to call her, no matter that he had no way of actually knowing that.

Tom wasn't the only one who was hung up on a girl at the Ferguson Farm, though.

Gene hadn't stopped thinking about Jessica since they'd left, but he couldn't bring himself to call. He was a total dick because it'd been his own fear that'd driven them apart.

Now, he wished they weren't so far away. It would take them most of the next day just to get to the depot, and it was even further to the girls'.

CHAPTER
FOUR

CHAPTER FOUR

*Jack

Jack shut off the lights of the truck as it rolled into the farmyard. The house was dark, as he expected.

There were two vehicles parked out front.

He recognized the red car from the bar.

"You sure about this?" Bill asked.

"Dude, she's a witch! She put a hex on me, I know it. All this bad crap that's been happening started when they arrived. Even Shelley disappearing."

Mentioning Shelly would be exactly what it took to get Bill's blood boiling. She'd been the girl Bill was sweet on until she went missing a few months ago.

They'd found her remains where the other missing people had been held captive near Lake George.

A lake that was on the Ferguson Farm property, where these two girls had just moved.

Bill had taken Shelley's death hard, even though she'd never shown an interest in him.

The official story that came out was that a rabid mountain lion had made a den in a cave near the lake, attacking anyone that came within range of the cave.

Something about the story had never sat right with Jack, but he hadn't been able to discover the truth.

He and Bill had often gone to Lake George to fish, and he'd seen no mountain lions. Then bodies started showing up when the witches moved in. They were probably using human sacrifices for their evil magic.

Bill ground his teeth as he got out of the truck and grabbed a tire iron out of the back of the cab, while Jack hefted a crowbar he'd brought along.

They crept up the stairs to the wrap-around porch at the front of the house. The top step creaked, and they both froze, listening for any sounds of movement in the house.

When they were confident no one had heard them, they approached the door.

It was unlocked.

Was it unlocked because they lived so far from town, or was it a streak of luck?

Not that it mattered.

They made their way up the interior stairs, as quietly as two drunk guys could.

They would pull the two girls out of bed and drag them outside to burn them at the stake.

Jack checked the bedrooms at the top of the stairs, finding only a storage room and what appeared to be a sewing room.

They moved on to the next set of rooms.

They each approached a door, counted to three, and then flung both doors open at the same time.

Jack flicked the lights on, and Bill followed suit, but they only found vacant beds.

"Where'd they go?" Bill asked.

"They gotta be here somewhere. Keep looking."

Jack and Bill searched the entire house but found no trace of either witch.

He screamed his anger and frustration and smashed up everything he could.

His friend soon joined him.

If they couldn't get back at the women physically, they sure would make a mess of their place.

Bill found a can of spray paint and graffitied several walls.

When they'd exhausted themselves, they left, leaving the house in disarray.

***Jessica**

Jessica was stuck in the dark, in the cold, in only her pajamas and her hoodie. She curled into a ball, holding the hoodie around her legs as much as she could.

She'd tried to find Alex, calling for her and feeling her way on her hands and knees, but she had no luck.

Jessica couldn't judge how long she'd been in the pitch black, and she was so turned around she had no way to find the door to open and get some light.

She felt up the walls for light switches but gave up when she remembered the other storm shelter had been a single cord in the middle of the room. She had no hope of finding it.

Why did Alex drag me down here?

Jessica had been having such a glorious dream, too, about being wrapped in Gene's arms. Now she was cold, sitting in the dirt alone.

Maybe Alex wasn't even in the room with her.

What if she shut me in here alone? No, she wouldn't have done that. She was right behind me. Why had she called me Edith?

Alex knew her legal name was Emily Jessica and that she

never used her first name, after a tragic situation with an old boyfriend.

But Edith?

Edith had been her great aunt. Jessica was her doppelgänger, and she'd never known. Alex had shown her the photo album, and she'd done some more digging.

She'd found out that her great-great-grandmother, Judith, had had two daughters, Edith and Barbara. It was their father, George, who had been found eaten by "animals."

Jessica and Alex had speculated that it was likely the Wendigo that Gene had killed. So, if it was her great-great-grandmother Judith who was haunting the place, then it had to have been Judith who had brought her down here.

Had she possessed Alex? How?

They both wore necklaces that were supposed to prevent stuff like that. It was supposed to protect them from possession of preternatural beings.

If it was Judith, what had she done with Alex and why were they even down here in the cold?

Jessica cried in the darkness, feeling helpless.

Why didn't I call Gene, like Alex told me to do weeks ago? If he was here, he'd find me. He'd found the Wendigo's lair, so surely he could find me.

She cried until she was completely exhausted. She curled up in a ball in the pitch black and fell asleep.

**Tom*

Tom was frantic by the time Gene pulled the old Ford Mustang into the farm the next evening. They'd been further away than he'd surmised, and he couldn't get there fast enough.

Gene had driven until his eyes burned and they traded driving duties.

Neither of them paid attention to their speed, pushing the vintage car harder than it had ever been before, only stopping when it needed to be refueled.

His cousin had taken over driving again a few hours later, reassuring Tom that he'd get them there as fast as he could.

Tom moved to the passenger seat, but he was no less anxious. They'd both only rested a small amount, not really sleeping, even though they both desperately needed a few good hours. He couldn't rest until he found Alex safe and sound.

From outside, the house looked normal.

They simultaneously scanned the upper windows for lights.

Tom was certain that Alex would've heard the car and run outside.

When neither girl appeared, his worry increased.

He and Gene approached the house cautiously.

His cousin lifted his hand to knock on the door, but it was unlatched.

Gene threw him a nod, and they both drew their guns.

They entered the house, smacking the nearest light switch.

It looked as if a tornado had hit the interior of the house. Everything appeared broken and strewn about.

"Alex!" Tom called as they moved through the debris toward the stairs.

At this time of night, the girls should've been in bed.

They raced up the stairs. The bedrooms were in worse shape than the rest of the house.

Die witches had been spray-painted on the stairwell and the bedroom walls.

Tom took in the surrounding chaos. There was no sign of Alex.

Where is she?

He checked under the bed and the closet in case she was hiding from whoever did this.

Then he saw it.

It was hanging off the edge of her laundry basket. The green dress she'd been wearing the first time he saw her and there was blood on it.

A lot of blood.

"Gene," Tom shouted, picking up the garment. He couldn't take his eyes off it.

"Shit," Gene said when he saw the dress. His cousin gestured to the room. "It looks like Jessica's room in here. Someone trashed it, too. But where the hell are the girls? There's no evidence they're even here! Except for the red Ford out front. Don't worry, we'll find them. Call Alex's phone."

Tom snatched his phone out to obey.

Her phone started ringing from the nightstand.

"Alex never goes anywhere without her phone." He swallowed and a cold chill of fear shot down his spine.

Gene dialed Jessica, and they followed the sound back to her room. Like Alex's, her phone was on the nightstand next to the bed.

"Where could they be?" his cousin asked, dropping onto the bed. "You don't think whoever did this took them, do you?"

Tom looked around Jessica's room. There was no trace of blood there. The covers on the bed looked as though someone had slept in them, but had had gotten up and left, rather than being dragged from the bed.

He closed his eyes and concentrated on Alex.

After several deep breaths, he headed out of the room.

Gene followed but didn't ask where he was going.

CHAPTER
FIVE

CHAPTER FIVE

**Tom*

Tom shot out of the house and around to the barn. He switched on the overhead lights. The place looked so different than when he'd last seen it. The dirt floor had been raked clean and someone had rebuilt the stalls. There was an enormous stack of hay on the right side of the building.

"Tom, where are you going?" Gene called but joined him in the barn.

"She's here somewhere." He checked the stalls.

"You think they were hiding out here, or that whoever did that?" Gene pointed to the house. "Or they were dragged out here and left?"

"I don't know. Just help me look."

They checked every nook and cranny, calling for the girls.

"Give me a sec," Gene said, climbing up the rickety ladder to the old loft. His cousin scanned the large barn. From the high vantage, he wouldn't miss any areas. "Ah, shit! How did we miss that?"

"What?" Tom asked, his heart speeding up, and dipping to his gut.

"Look over there, in the back of the barn." Gene indicated an area where a large shelf was knocked over, its contents spilled everywhere. "Do you see the door there?"

Tom ran a hand through his hair that was long enough to brush his shoulders. "Gene, there isn't a door here. But there has to be something I'm not seeing. I don't know how to explain this, but I feel her right here." He stomped his foot to emphasize, and a hollow sound rang out.

"That's what I'm talking about!" his cousin said, hurrying down the ladder to join him.

They found the handle and lifted it up.

"Alex!" Tom called.

"Jessica!" Gene echoed.

"Gene?" a small voice called from the darkness.

His cousin ran down the ramp, pulling his phone out and flicking on the flashlight.

Tom found the kickstand that held the door open and then followed. The light from Gene's phone was coming from his left.

"Are they here?"

"I just found Jess," Gene replied. "Jess? Where's Alex?"

"I don't know! It was so dark." Her voice was shaking.

"Get her inside to warm up," Tom said, "I'll keep looking."

"I'm not leaving until you find her," Jessica screeched.

"Please, get inside. She'd be pissed if she knew I let you stay out here when you clearly need to go warm up," Tom pushed.

He watched her nod in agreement, as Gene carried her out of the barn.

He shone his flashlight around the large room. It wrapped on either side of the ramp with horse stalls on one side and old bags of feed on the other. Dirt and cobwebs covered the whole place.

It looked like no one had been in there in over a hundred years. Tom opened the closest stall and shone his light inside. He cursed and closed his eyes when he spotted a skeleton.

It couldn't be Alex, but that didn't mean his heart didn't skip.

The clothes were from the turn of the century, and he had a good idea who it was.

He whirled away, stepping out of the stall. Alex was crumpled up against the right side of the ramp.

"Alex!" Tom rushed to her and rolled her over. His heart was slamming in his chest. She wasn't moving. His deepest fear, her death, washed over him.

Her body was cool to the touch and her eyes were closed, so he checked for a pulse.

Her heartbeat was there and rapid.

Thank God.

"Alex?" he said, gently cradling her face in his hand. "Alex, please wake up."

She didn't respond.

Tom scooped her up and carried her up the ramp.

He needed to warm her up and check her over for injuries. He strode past Gene and Jessica, who was by the car and headed for the house.

"Alex!" Jessica cried. "Is she alright?"

"Let me get her inside, I need better light to check her out."

Tom made his way into the house, Jessica on his heels, practically clawing him to make sure her best friend was alright.

Tom laid Alex on the couch in the living room.

She was still shivering, so he pulled the blanket off the back to cover her.

He took her face in his hand again, gently patting her cheek. "Alex, wake up," ordered.

Her eyes remained closed.

He ran a hand through her hair and ran into a sticky mess that had his breath catching. His fingers were covered in drying blood.

"Tom! Is that blood?" the other woman cried.

He quickly turned her face away from him to look at the back of her head. It was hard to tell the exact injury, because her hair was so matted with blood.

He jumped up and dashed to the kitchen. He soaked a hand towel in warm water and returned to Alex. He had to push Jessica out of the way, she was gripping Alex's hand with such force, that her knuckles were white.

Tom rolled her onto her side so he could clean the back of her head easier.

A gash ran from the top of her left ear to the middle of the back of her head. It continued to ooze as he wiped the blood away.

It was shallow, thank God, but head wounds bled like a bitch.

He'd stitched up worse on himself and Gene, but he needed a needle and thread.

Jessica's sewing room!

Not wanting to leave his love, he turned to his cousin. "Can you run up to Jessica's sewing room and grab some thread and a sewing needle?"

"On it," Gene replied.

Tom could hear his cousin take the stairs two at a time, his long legs making quick work of the staircase.

Waiting for Gene to return, Tom took a full inventory of the one room. His blood boiled as he thought of what he'd do to the people who did this.

How could people think that they were witches?

Alex had told him they kept to themselves on the farm. They went to the bigger towns to go shopping, but she never talked about spending any time in Broken Bow.

Gene returned with scissors, needles, and thread.

Tom smiled at the pink spool in his hand. He held it up to Gene. "Really? Pink?"

"Yeah. I remember Jessica saying one it was Alex's favorite color." His cousin turned to Jessica. "Let's get you taken care of."

"I don't want to leave her side," she cried.

"I know, but you really don't want to watch Tom stitch her up. It's pretty gross."

Jessica let out a sigh. "Maybe we should call 911?"

"NO!" Gene said adamitly. "You know how we feel about cops. Besides, we have dealt with worse on ourselves. She'll be fine by morning."

Tom appreciated the help from his cousin. The moment they were out of the room, he stitched up her head. He made smaller careful stitches than he normally would. He didn't want her to have a big scar because he did a sloppy job.

When he was done, he washed as much of the blood out of Alex's hair as he could with the towel and tossed everything on the coffee table. He pulled her up to a sitting position and sat behind her, pulling her into his lap. He wrapped the blanket around them to trap his body heat in and help warm her up.

It felt good to have her in his arms again.

Now if she'd just wake up...

Gene

Gene walked slowly behind Jessica, reliving the last few minutes over in his mind. He'd followed the sound of Jessica's voice in the barn, trying to find his way in the limited light. She wasn't wearing much. She had a hoodie on, so her arms were covered, but her legs were bare.

She was off to the left side of the ramp, crouched in a corner, shivering.

"Are you hurt?" he demanded, trying to look her over with his flashlight.

"No, just cold. So cold that my body's stiff. It's hard to move," she said, through chattering teeth.

It wasn't particularly cold out yet, despite it being the end of November, but being in her pajamas in a dark, damp space must've dropped her body temperature significantly.

Gene scooped her up and carried her up the ramp. He sat her on the warm hood of his prized vehicle. He cupped her face as he examined her.

Tears flowed down her cheeks. "You saved me, just like I knew you would. But how? How did you find me?" she cried.

"Tom knew something was wrong, so we headed straight here. What happened, Jessica?"

"It was Judith. I think she possessed Alex, but I don't know how."

"Judith? Who's Judith?" Gene asked, frowning.

"She's our ghost. Remember, my great-great-grams. The one you forgot to help cross over when you left in such a hurry."

He shook his head, trying not to recall that night. He'd made the biggest mistake of his life that night. "No, a ghost shouldn't have been able to possess Alex, not if she was wearing the protection charm." He was relieved to see the necklace hanging around Jessica's neck. He lifted it from the swell of her breasts, the limited heat from her body warming the circle of flames slightly. Gene dropped the charm, and pulled her into his embrace, rubbing his hands up and down her back to help warm her up. "I'm so sorry, Jessica. I wasn't here for you," he whispered into her chestnut hair.

Jessica started sobbing when Tom carried an obviously unconscious Alex to the house. She stood up, determined to follow and Gene put her arm around her to support her.

It only took a few steps for him to realize Jessica was barefoot. He stopped and picked her up.

She studied his face as he held her against him. "You came for me," she repeated.

Gene shook his head to bring him back to the moment.

"You came for me," rang through his body. He stepped suddenly into the library so they could talk alone. He set her on the sofa and sat next to her, facing her. He caressed her cheek and buried his fingers in her long thick hair. His left hand held her right hand. He swallowed to gather courage before he spoke. "Jessica, I shouldn't have left. When I realized what you meant to me, I had to leave. It was the only way I could protect you."

"Alex said you had a case."

He shook his head and averted his gaze. He didn't have the balls to look at her. "There's always a case, but I knew if I stuck around, something bad would happen to you." When he met her eyes again, hers were misty. "I just couldn't bear that."

"Bullshit!" Jessica pulled away and scrambled to her feet. "You told me I was everything you ever wanted, then you ran away as fast as you could."

"I didn't—" he huffed out a breath.

That was *exactly* what he'd done.

Like a fucking coward.

"If you don't want me, fine. But don't keep Tom away from Alex. She loves him."

"I do want you, Jess," Gene admitted. "But you know my lifestyle. We are on the go all the time. We are lucky to spend a few days a month at home."

"Then why bother coming back now?" she asked, this time more calmly.

"Tom said you needed us. I thought maybe a demon had gotten to you."

"A demon? Seriously? Those are real, too?" Her aquamarine eyes were wide, and her tempting mouth half-agape.

"And so much more. But it's all right, I won't let them hurt you," he said, reaching for her, but she scooted away, and Gene let his hands drop to his lap.

"Does this mean you're gonna leave again?" Jessica asked, tears streaming down her cheeks.

"I don't know," he said, standing up and falling into an agitated pace. "I want to be with you, but people who are close to me tend to get hurt. The best thing I can do for you is leave so you can live your life." He paused with his back to her and ran his hand over his neck and over the back of his head. He wanted to cuss and scream, and bare his heart—or run the fuck away.

She crossed the room to him. Jessica pressed herself to his back, wrapping her arms around him. "Please don't go," she whispered. "I don't think I could handle it if you left again."

Gene turned and pulled her against him.

She was still cold from spending most of the day under the barn.

He wrapped his arms around her, rubbing circles on her back to help warm her up.

CHAPTER
SIX

CHAPTER SIX

Jessica had woken up alone on the sofa. Gene had left her again. Tears filled her eyes and spilled over.

She should just go upstairs. When she made it to her feet, voices in the kitchen caught her attention. She tiptoed down the hall, stopping just out of view. Tom and Gene were talking quietly. A sigh of relief floated past her lips.

He *hadn't* left her.

"Is it working?" Tom's sleepy voice came first. "I could really use some coffee."

Something was being moved around.

"The damned coffee maker was in the sink. What the fuck did they hit it with?" Gene's voice was filled with anger.

"Maybe a baseball bat?" Tom said.

Jessica guessed at the sounds she heard. She stayed where she was, picturing things in the kitchen. She didn't want them to know, just yet, that she was awake and listening.

She knew what Gene was doing. She'd gotten used to his morning routine when the guys had stayed with them before. Put water in the pot, transfer to the machine, load the basket with coffee, and start it brewing.

Jessica smiled when the smell filled the house.

"How is Alex?" Gene asked.

Tom gave a loud sigh. "She's still unconscious. She took an impact to the back of the head, and I had to stitch her up."

The moment Jessica heard her friend was still unconscious, she felt sick to her stomach, the pain so overwhelming she doubled over. It took her a few strong breaths to stand upright again, still listening to the cousins speaking.

"How did that happen? According to Jessica, the girls were in the storm shelter before whoever did this damage showed up."

"I don't know. She hit her head on something. I don't think someone hit her on the head."

"I don't know either but I tell you what, when I find the people responsible for this mess I'm gonna have a few choice things to say to them. And I may not be using words," Gene said, still sounding really angry.

Jessica interpreted this as they weren't leaving soon. Her heart leaped, and she chided herself not to get carried away, considering she still had a secret Gene didn't know.

But that joy faded as fast as it had arrived.

Alex was still in danger.

She stepped into the kitchen, her shoulders pulled back with authority. "Hello, boys."

Gene turned to look at her, deep concern etched in his deep green eyes.

"How are you feeling?" he asked.

"I'm cold. But fine. It's Alex I am worried about."

Tom stepped up to her, putting his large hands on her shoulders. "You have to trust us, Jess. We have been through this before. She'll be fine. She just needs rest."

"Baby, why don't you try having a hot shower? Might help."

She knew she wasn't going to get her way in this, so she turned back down the hall and headed upstairs. Maybe a hot shower and some real clothes were the answer to feeling better. She was still cold.

She gasped when she saw the words spray-painted on the hallway wall. "Die Witches."

Jessica had seen the damage on the main floor of the house but didn't expect it to be upstairs, too. She checked in every room and only found damage.

The intruders had trashed everything breakable. She couldn't hold back more tears as she saw all the things she and Alex held dear destroyed, including her sewing machine.

It was all just too much.

Jessica sat down on the edge of her bed. Her phone was sitting on the nightstand where she'd set it last night before falling asleep.

It wasn't just about Alex still being out, it was so much more. Jessica knew it was time to call for help.

The night they'd rescued the people from the Wendigo, the sheriff had given her his personal cellphone number and said if she ever needed anything to call him.

The phone rang twice before a man's groggy voice.

"Sheriff Wilson? It's Jessica Remington. I'm sorry to call you this early, but I need your help."

"Of course, little lady. And please call me Jasper. What can I help you with this Thanksgiving morning?"

Jessica had completely forgotten about the holiday. They'd been so wrapped up in learning to live on the farm, it hadn't crossed her mind. However, there were other more important things to worry about.

She explained most of the details about their house being ransacked without mentioning the ghost. She'd learned when the Wendigo situation had happened that Tom and Gene did not do well around the police, so Jessica asked the sheriff to come alone as a personal favor.

He explained he just needed a cuppa Joe, and he'd be on his way.

The sheriff was far enough from the farm that she'd have enough time to take a shower.

Jessica quietly shut the door to the bathroom and turned on the water. She was grateful that for once, the pipes didn't creak and groan. While the water heated, she told her cell to shuffle her music. She hung her hoodie on the door handle and stripped out of her pajamas to enjoy the warm water of the shower.

She began singing along to the song *Lost in Love* by Air Supply.

Jessica heard the door open and close and stuck her head around the curtain.

Gene was standing there.

Her heart thundered in her chest. This was NOT how she wanted him to find out.

She was careful to keep the curtain pulled closed, so she didn't expose any part of her body. If he'd noticed she'd put on a few pounds when he'd carried her, she was grateful he hadn't commented. Her breasts had gone up over one cup size already.

"Can you hand me that towel there?" She gestured with her head, toward the towel hanging on the back of the door.

"I thought maybe you might like some company." He smiled seductively.

"I'm just getting out."

Gene grabbed the towel, shaking his head, and not hiding his disappointment. He was whispering, so low Jessica had to strain to be sure she heard him right.

"I know every inch of your body intimately. Why are you suddenly so shy?" He handed her the towel. "Are you all right?" he asked in a normal tone, as if he'd not just spoken his feelings aloud.

"I'm fine." Jessica snatched the towel and quickly wrapped it around herself, just as he wrenched the curtains open. She hunched over slightly to hide any evidence he might see. "I said I'm fine, but I've got to get dressed, Gene. Sheriff Wilson will be here any minute. Can you please show him what happened?"

"You called the cops? Jessica! You know we can't get wrapped up in police crap!" A frown marred his handsome face.

Jessica hugged the towel a little tighter. His anger spiked hers and she glared. "No shit, Gene! That's why I asked him to come alone. Now will you please go watch for him so I can get dressed?"

Gene glared right back, his face turning red. "I don't understand you! You held on to me like you'd never let go, then completely pushed me away. Fine. I'm better off without you anyway." He whirled and left, his boots echoing as he stormed down the stairs.

She stared. Then blinked, and her face burned with anger and embarrassment. Not to mention, hurt.

He was acting like a spoiled, selfish child.

She wanted to retaliate, but that was exactly what he was doing. Gene had pushed her away when he didn't understand things.

She let out a sigh and stepped out of the bathtub.

She dried off and hung her damp towel. Something on a chain caught her eye.

Alex's protection charm.

Jessica quickly dressed in leggings and an oversized sweatshirt, grabbing the necklace off the hook by the mirror, then headed downstairs.

The guys were still in the kitchen, talking through the swinging bar doors.

"I know how she did it," Jessica said. "Alex left her necklace in the bathroom after her bath." She held the necklace up.

Tom took it. He ran the thumb over the unicursal hexagram in the center. "Why did she take it off? It won't tarnish in the water. It's silver. If Alex makes it through this, I'm going to insist she get the symbol tattooed."

Jessica laughed. "Well, Tom. I hope you plan on holding her down to have it done. Alex said there was nothing in the world important enough to her to mark up her body. She's all for other people having them, but never wants a tattoo for herself."

"We will see," Tom's said, his expression unreadable.

CHAPTER
SEVEN

CHAPTER SEVEN

Jessica

Tom headed into the living room, Alex's necklace in hand. He sat on the coffee table across from her bestie and he fastened the necklace around her neck.

She looked as if she was just asleep but she should've woken when Tom moved her.

Jessica wanted to scream at the situation. She was trying to have faith in the cousins, but this was her best friend. She felt like they weren't taking Alex's situation seriously.

There was a knock at the front door, and Jessica dashed over. It was better if she met the sheriff, and not Gene or Tom. "Thanks for coming, Sheriff." She stepped to the side, so the older man could enter.

"Of course. I'm glad to see you back here as well, son," Sheriff Wilson said to Gene.

They shook hands, and for someone who didn't like cops, Gene seemed relaxed.

"I think I'm gonna have to convince you boys to stick around and help me keep an eye on these girls. Trouble seems to follow them," The lawman said.

"You have no idea," Gene muttered under his breath.

Jessica shot him a silent glare.

The sheriff surveyed the house, obviously taking in the destruction.

"Boy, you weren't a kiddin' about being vandalized!" he said, walking further into the house.

"I think it was that guy from the bar," Jessica said.

"You weren't here when this happened?" the sheriff asked.

Jessica glanced at Gene. Could—or should—she mention they were in some sort of old-fashioned panic room in the barn?

"They heard a ruckus and hid in the barn," Gene said.

She sucked in a breath and nodded.

"I see. I expect it was those boys, but I need proof."

"You know who did this?" Gene asked, anger reddening his face.

"I'd say this is retaliation for the trouble they got into at the bar."

"What happened at the bar?" Gene asked, catching Jessica's eye. Then he looked back at the sheriff. "Why would they come here?"

"Because we were there," Jessica said. "That Jack guy was harassing Alex."

"What about Alex?" Tom asked.

"What happened to Alex?" The sheriff asked, walking right into the living room. "I thought you said you girls weren't here when they showed up?"

"She hit her head and hasn't woken up yet," Tom said, not looking up.

"When was this?" the older man asked, looking back at Jessica. "Did those boys do this?" He cleared his throat as if he was trying to keep cool, as a cop should, but his face was red, too. The sheriff was mad.

"Tom found her last night," Gene said. "Alex and Jess had hidden in a storm shelter when they heard trouble coming."

Sheriff Wilson looked to Jessica for confirmation.

She nodded. "She hit her head going into the storm shelter."

"I think we'd best get her to the hospital," he said, pulling out his phone.

"I couldn't agree more," Jessica pushed. "I've been saying that all along."

"Alex hates hospitals," Tom said, trying to convince the sheriff not to call. "I'm keeping an eye on her. Not my first unconscious person."

Sheriff Wilson clearly disagreed. He red in his cheeks said what his words didn't. He let out a huff and turned to Jessica. "We need to get you seen by a doctor, too."

"Maybe the sheriff is right?" Gene asked, glancing at his cousin. "We should've taken them to the hospital last night."

"Thank you," Jessica murmured under her breath.

Tom ran a hand over his face in obvious exhaustion. "I guess you're right. She's not waking up and I don't know why."

"Finally." Jessica sighed.

"But no ambulance." Tom pointed out.

"I guess I could get you there faster than if we waited for the medics," the sheriff said. "And you'll get checked out, too, missy."

It was the best Jessica was gonna get, so she agreed. She was still cold, but she'd warm up in time; she wasn't worried about it. The baby should get checked. She just had to figure out how to keep Gene out of the room.

———

Jessica sat in the passenger's seat of the Mustang, and Gene drove to town, following the sheriff. She kept her hand on his thigh but couldn't put her finger on whether it was to keep him calm or herself.

She had to figure out how to tell him about the baby before he found out from the doctor. HIPAA wasn't going to save her or ban him from her room. He would insist on being with her.

Any other time, she might be grateful if he was that sweet.

Right now?

Not so much.

Her heart thundered in her ears, and she swallowed as she reached for courage and ordered herself to open her mouth. "Gene, I need to tell you something," she whispered.

"Yes, you do. Why didn't you call us if you were being harassed?" He asked but kept his eyes on the road.

Her temper flared. "Why would I call *you*? You *left*, remember?"

"You could've had Alex call Tom," he barked, his voice defensive.

She gasped, and bit her lip to control her anger. How dare he turn this back on her?

Jessica had nothing more to say. She folded her arms and looked out the window as they sped through town, following the sheriff.

Tom was visible in the back seat of the sheriff's car. He was holding her best friend tight in his arms.

She hated that she wasn't with her friend, but it'd proved too difficult to get an unconscious person in the back seat of a two-door car.

When they arrived at the small county hospital, there was a gurney and a wheelchair waiting.

Sheriff Wilson must have called their arrival in.

Tom looked disgruntled, as the medical team pushed him to the side.

They gently retrieved and laid Alex on the gurney.

"All right, let's get you in this wheelchair, young lady. You need a checkup, too," Sheriff Wilson said guiding Jessica over to the wheelchair.

"No, thank you," she said. "I'm fine."

"You will sit your ass in that chair, or I will put you in it," Gene said in a very gravelly voice that sent goosebumps up into her hairline and made her nether regions quiver.

Not now! Stupid hormones!

"I can walk just fine. I don't need to sit," she huffed.

"Please," Gene finally said.

That was certainly the first time he'd pleaded with her to do something.

He was the most gorgeous man she'd ever met, with his green eyes, short brown hair, and those long legs…

Jessica had to shake her head to get her mind off of things that made her body react against her will. Her hormones had made her a spicy disaster when it came to all things of a sexual nature.

She finally agreed to sit in the wheelchair and agreed to go inside for a checkup.

Gene followed her to her little cubicle in the Emergency Department. He sat with her while they waited for someone to come in.

A medical assistant came in and checked Jessica into the computer system.

She took her temperature.

Jessica frowned at the surprised look on her face as she entered it into the computer.

"Your temperature is low," the woman commented.

She took her blood pressure next. Another shocked look registered on her face. She quickly removed the cuff. "The doctor should be right in," she said quickly and left.

However, the next person in wasn't a doctor, it was a phlebotomist. She said nothing, just drew three vials of blood and left.

Jessica's heart pounded. There was no mystery as to what her blood would say.

This was not how she wanted Gene to find out.

Her leg bobbed up and down of its own accord, and her gut clenched.

Was something wrong with the baby?

Gene hadn't seen the look on the medical assistant's face. He'd been focused on his phone.

"Gene?" Jessica whispered.

He looked up at her, arching an eyebrow.

"What is it?" she asked.

"It's nothing, just a friend who thinks there might be a job for us," he admitted.

"Do you have to leave?" Jessica asked, a knot forming in her stomach.

"No, it can wait," Gene said, reaching for her hand.

She was relieved that he would stay but still didn't know how to tell him she was carrying his child. "Can you please go check on Alex? At least let Tom know where we are," she said, instead of what she should have confessed.

Gene came to the bed. He kissed her forehead softly. "She's right, you know, you are a bit cold. Do you need another blanket?"

His concern warmed her, but she felt hot enough at the moment. "No, I'm fine. But please, can you go check on Alex? I'm really worried."

His expression shouted that he was reluctant to leave, but he went.

The moment he was out of sight, Jessica let out a sigh of relief. It only lasted a moment before the doctor came in, followed by a nurse and the medical assistant.

"Miss Remington, I'm Dr. Pan. How are you feeling today?"

"I'm fine, really. I tried telling them I didn't need to be seen."

Dr. Pan stepped up closer to the bed, reaching for her hand and checking her pulse. After he timed her with his wristwatch, he reached for her forehead. "Well, according to your blood work, there are a few things we need to be concerned about."

Jessica nodded. Surely, he was speaking of her baby. She had yet to feel the flutters of the baby's movement that she had read about in her baby book. Her baby was the only reason she was willing to be in the hospital bed. "I guess you're right. We really should check on the baby."

The doctor whipped around in a flurry to look at the nurse behind him. "Baby?"

Her heart fluttered. "Isn't that what you're talking about? That the bloodwork showed I was pregnant? Is everything all right with my baby?" Her hands went instinctively to her small mound.

"If you'll please excuse us. There is something we need to verify." The doctor escorted his colleagues out of the room.

Panic inched up from her gut, throwing her heart into a canter.

If they weren't concerned because of her baby, what was going on?

Jessica wouldn't get answers immediately.

The nurse came back into the room with a small cart. Without speaking to Jessica, she put a rather large needle into the top of her hand to administer fluids through an IV.

A flurry of people then proceeded to come into the room, wanting to get papers for her to sign for admittance and others getting the gurney she was on ready to be moved. No one would give her a straight answer, only that she was being admitted and taken to a room.

"Will someone please tell me what the hell is going on?"

They ignored her and she was pushed down the hallway on the gurney.

"Seriously? Can't you give me a straight answer?"

Finally, the person pushing the bed replied. "You're being admitted. That's all I know."

Jessica's heart was in her throat, pounding harder and harder with the fear that was building.

Why had she sent Gene away?

She didn't want him to find out they were having a baby this way, but she was scared and didn't want to be alone.

They got her into a room and transferred her from one bed to another.

As soon as the orderly left with the emergency department

gurney, a technician came in pushing with her a portable ultrasound machine.

Once the lady got everything set up, she put the warm gel on Jessica's belly and hummed quietly to herself.

"Is everything all right?" she asked, her voice shaky.

"Oh, I'm sure everything's fine, sweetie. They just called me up to do a quick ultrasound and check on your little one. Do you know how far along you are?"

Her breath came a little easier at the woman's soft voice and calm demeanor.

The ultrasound tech was very kind and not rushing about like the doctor and nurses had been. She wasn't acting at all like there was any problem.

"I'm about twenty weeks along." Jessica swallowed and sucked in air, in anticipation of seeing her growing child for the first time. She'd heard the heartbeat a few times but wasn't scheduled for her first ultrasound for a while.

The baby's heartbeat filled the silence in the room, a beautiful staccato with strength and life.

The technician rolled the wand around the gel on her belly, and they were both looking at a white, black, and gray blurry image on the monitor.

She didn't quite understand what they were looking at, until the technician stopped it in one spot.

It was a clear outline of the baby's head.

The technician continued to observe every aspect of the growing child. Pointing out what were the fingers and spine and, most importantly, the intensely beating heart.

"Your baby looks wonderful. A very strong heartbeat, good-looking spine, and all the important things in the right places."

"Is there any chance of finding out about my baby's sex?" Jessica asked.

"Unfortunately, not yet. We could get a general idea, but half the time we are wrong. It's just not a clear enough view yet." The tech printed out a handful of images and handed them to Jessica before wheeling the machine out of the room.

She stared at the blurry images of her baby.

Gene's child.

She put her hand over her growing womb and whispered as much to the baby as herself.

"I hope your daddy doesn't leave us again. We need him."

So did so many others.

Was Jessica being selfish for wanting Gene to be there for her and their child?

Or did she need to finally find a way to say goodbye forever?

CHAPTER
EIGHT

CHAPTER EIGHT

Gene

Gene's frustration was going to eat him alive. He just wanted to return to Jessica, but this small-town hospital was either very short-staffed, or busy with someone else's emergency.

He had seen no one other than an ancient security guard who wouldn't let him leave the waiting area once he had entered the space.

A staff member, who promised to find out where his cousin was, left him there after saying they would promptly return.

Which they hadn't.

Gene was so used to having free rein in the hospital when he and his cousin were usually posing as FBI agents. However, as an average guy, he was so helpless.

All he wanted to know was what room Alex was in, but he didn't know her last name, so they shot him down.

He tried to both call and text Tom but was being ignored.

Gene got it. Had it been Jessica that was unconscious, he

would've been the same, but it didn't stop him from getting frustrated.

The lady wasn't coming back soon, so he was wasting his time in the lobby. He headed back toward Jessica and the room she had in the ED.

The door to the space he'd left her in was open, but the curtains were drawn.

He stepped in and peeked around the pale blue fabric, but Jessica wasn't there.

A young girl sat in the bed, with a woman he assumed was her mother standing beside her.

Gene apologized and stepped out, shaking his head. Maybe he'd gone to the wrong room. He looked up and down the hallway. It'd been the correct room, down the hall on the left from the nurse's station.

He hurried back up the hall, his heart in his throat.

Finally, someone had returned.

He forgot his search for his cousin; Jessica, was his only concern.

"Where the hell did Jessica go? Where did they move her to?" His patience was wearing thin, and he was really worried. Unfamiliar emotions darted around in his chest.

"What's the last name?"

He didn't know it.

How could he not even know her last name?

"She was in room six down there and now she's gone," Gene growled.

The nurse barely looked up from her computer screen when replying to him. "Unless you're immediate family, well, you shouldn't even be here."

He puffed up, standing a bit taller and pulling his shoulders back. "I'm practically immediate family! She's my… My… My Jessica!"

The nurse just looked at him with one eyebrow raised. "Seriously? Do you know how many times I hear that daily? Nice try." She turned back to the computer she'd been tapping away at.

When he still couldn't get any information out of her, he raised his voice. "I will go room to room disturbing everyone if you don't tell me where Jessica was moved to!"

Before Gene enacted the threat, the doctor that'd seen Jessica came appeared and pulled him aside. Concern was all over the older man's face. "You came in here with Miss Jessica Remington, correct?"

Remington, like the gun?

"Yeah. Where the hell is she?" Gene didn't mean to be so surly with the doctor, he was just beyond frustrated.

"Come with me." The doctor walked away from the Emergency Department, toward the main corridor of the hospital.

Gene followed right beside him.

"I apologize for not properly introducing myself. I'm Doctor Michael Pan."

"Gene Priest," he replied, shaking the older man's hand.

"We admitted Miss Remington and placed her in a room," the doctor said. "We started IV fluids because she's severely dehydrated. But we had a few anomalies in her blood work and we're hoping you could help us clarify a few things."

"What do you mean by anomalies?" Gene asked.

"Some of the discrepancy makes sense because of her current condition. But a few things are really throwing us for a loop. Can you tell us exactly what happened in the past 48 hours?" Dr. Pan stopped just outside of a patient's room with the door shut.

Gene did his best to explain what little he knew, primarily highlighting that she'd been locked in the storm shelter for almost twenty-four hours. She had very little clothing, no light, and definitely no food or water.

"That explains why her body temperature is low. It should rise since she's under a warming blanket right now. It's dangerous for anyone's body temperature to drop below 96, but especially one in her condition."

He cocked his head to one side.

Condition?

That was the second time the doctor had said something regarding the shape Jessica was in. However, no one was clarifying what that meant.

"Her body temperature shouldn't still be that low, should it?" he asked. "We wrapped her up to warm her as soon as we found her and she had a hot shower this morning. It should've done the trick, shouldn't it?"

"Generally, yes it should. Last night was the first frost of the year and temperatures dropped rather low. If she was in the storm shelter, it could've gotten chilly in there."

Gene nodded. Then he remembered something the doctor had said about her blood. "So doc, what else seems to be going on? You said you had other concerns…"

The doctor leaned a little closer, like he didn't want any passersby of this tiny hospital to overhear what he said. "Her blood pressure was way too low. Between you and me, with her low body temperature and her low heart rate and her white blood cell count being completely inadequate, this girl should not be alive. In her condition, her white blood count should be elevated. The stress and dehydration alone should have sent it through the roof."

He took a step back so he could look the doctor in the face. "What are you saying? I don't understand. Is the same thing going on with Alex?"

Dr. Pan was quiet for a minute, like he was contemplating how much information he should share. "You're lucky. Sheriff Wilson said you boys were to be treated like immediate family, but it is still against the hospital policy to divulge any personal information to non-immediate family without consulting the patient first." He let out a deep breath. "But with one unconscious and the other about to be sedated, I feel it is only right to bypass policies."

"Thank God for small favors," Gene mumbled.

"But to answer your question, no. Miss Springfield is something entirely different. Her body temperature is fine, her heart rate is normal for someone sleeping. We can't understand why she is currently unconscious."

He could tell the older gentleman was struggling.

The man took off his gold-wired glasses and cleaned them with a cloth from his white jacket. "We're just a small county hospital here, sir, so we have sent in a request for a portable EKG monitor to be sent from North Platte. It makes little sense for us to move either of them to another hospital when it will be faster to bring the equipment here. Especially since we are about to sedate Miss Remington to see if it will help with her heart rate." He opened the door and allowed Gene to step in before he turned and walked away.

Sure enough, at that moment, a nurse was putting a syringe into Jessica's IV line.

"Hey, baby," Gene said, stepping up to the bed and putting a hand on her forehead.

They had her covered in silver foil. A warming blanket. Trying to bring her body temperature up.

He wished they'd just let him curl up on the bed next to her and heat her up himself.

Jessica looked up at him, but her blue-green eyes were already glazing over. Within a few moments, her eyes fluttered and shut.

"The medication we gave her will cause her to sleep, most likely only a few hours, but enough to see if her heart rate will change in a relaxed and sleeping state. We're going to leave the warming blankets on, but I will be back to check on her in a little while." Dr. Pan nodded as he stepped out.

The nurse showed Gene how to use the call button if he had any concerns.

Since she seemed to be more on the friendly side, Gene put on his charm, giving her a crooked smile.

"Can you possibly give me an update on Alex? It's Jessica's best friend. And if she wakes and I don't have an update, I'm worried she's gonna have a meltdown. And I'm sure none of us want that."

"Oh, um. I'm not sure. Let me see what I can find out, But I can't make any promises." She nodded, her expression open and earnest.

"I get that," he murmured. "Anything you can tell me will help. My cousin's with her, but he's not answering his phone, not even replying to texts."

"I'll do my best." The nurse winked and slipped from the room.

Gene watched as Jessica's chest moved up and down in slow, rhythmic breathing. He couldn't tear his eyes away, assuring himself she had to be okay.

He finally looked up, checked the monitors she was attached to, and watched the beat of her heart go up and down.

Gene didn't know what a normal blood pressure reading was so all he could do was watch the numbers fluctuate.

They'd tucked her arms under the warming blanket and it was pulled up to her neck.

All Gene could see was her head.

He needed to touch her.

Needed to be connected.

Gene lifted the corner of the warming blanket and slipped a hand underneath to find Jessica's.

If all he could do was hold her hand while she slept at least it was something. When his hand located hers, he found it wasn't empty.

She had something in her grip.

He lifted the blanket higher to see some paper rolled up and grasped between her fingers and thumb.

Gene gently removed it from her hand and began unrolling the paper.

It was images.

It didn't click what exactly he was looking at, until he noticed the words on the paper.

Head.

Hand.

Heart.

He swallowed when it smacked into him.

Bits and pieces of what the doctor had just told him came flooding back.

Her *condition.*

Her blood work didn't make sense.

She shouldn't be alive.

Is Jessica really pregnant?

Is she going to die?

What then fuck was he supposed to do now?

What would an average Joe do in a situation like this?

Pray.

So Gene did just that.

CHAPTER
NINE

CHAPTER NINE

Tom

Tom paced the hallway.

They'd admitted Alex almost immediately and moved her into a room. They hadn't let him see her while they ran all their tests, mostly because the room was so small and there were several people coming and going.

He leaned against the wall opposite her door and waited.

Tom slid down the wall to sit on the floor. He wrapped his arms around his legs and dropped his head between his arms.

"Sir?" An older man stood in front of him. "You can see her now."

Tom climbed to his feet. He was exhausted. "Is she awake?"

"Not yet."

The nurse was still making notes on the computer when he entered the room.

He walked around the bed and sat in the chair next to Alex.

The doctor offered his hand. "I'm Dr. Gibbons."

"Tom Priest."

"Are you related?"

Since the doctor couldn't give him any answers unless he was family, Tom had to think fast. Then, his eyes landed on the doctor's. The man was twisting his wedding ring with his left thumb.

"Fiancé," he finally answered. No doubt his desperation was visible on his face, and the doctor could see—and sense—what was between him, Tom, and Alex.

"Well, her vitals are strong. That's a good start. She suffered a severe concussion, but the swelling is going down and she should wake up soon."

"How long?"

"Honestly, I'm surprised she hasn't woken up yet," the doctor said. "But it's hard to tell with head injuries. I'll be checking back on her. You're welcome to stay with her. Just hit the call button here on the bed if she comes to."

"Thank you, Doctor."

Once the man left, Tom moved closer to the bed. He needed contact with her. His soul called to hers, he felt it from the inside out. He gently ran his fingertips down her cheek, feeling the heat of her skin, bringing their connection closer.

Gene

Gene bowed his head over the pictures in his hand. "I don't know if anyone's listening, but if you are..." he spoke aloud. "I really could use your help. I've never asked for help, but I don't know what to do."

Was there such a thing as angels?

Or...God?

There were definitely demons, reapers, and just about every monster ever written in fiction books.

God and angels…he'd never come across anything to say if they were real.

Now was the time to see if they were.

Would they come if he pleaded with them?

Gene looked around, hoping someone would appear. When they didn't, he tried again. "Please! I can't lose her…them."

He groaned and clenched his jaw.

Nothing was happening…but wasn't that only natural?

Only four months ago, he'd seen his first Fayefolk.

Wait.

Maybe that was who he needed to pray to—the Faye. They'd saved his cousin.

Why not ask them to save the woman he loved?

The door opening scattered his thoughts, and plan to pray to the Faye.

"I'm sorry to bother you, but I found out where your cousin and friend are," the nurse from earlier said. "They're just a few doors down, around the corner."

Gene didn't want to leave Jessica alone, but she'd want answers when she finally came to. He patted her hand gently and followed the nurse out into the hallway.

When he got to Alex's room, Tom was sitting in a chair next to the bed Alex was lying on, his face buried in his hands.

Gene knew how he felt.

So hopeless.

It almost made him laugh at the irony of it all.

He put a hand on his cousin's shoulder.

Tom looked up at him, his eyes so stormy.

"Any news?" Gene asked.

Tom just shook his head. "They said her vitals are strong. They're not sure why she's still out. It's like she's just sleeping." His cousin sounded so forlorn, as he looked over at the girl that had changed his life. "I can't lose her," he whispered.

Gene completely understood.

Tom looked back at Gene. "How's Jessica taking all this? I thought they'd check her out and she'd want to be in here."

Tears burned his eyes—but he couldn't cry like that. Not even in front of his cousin. He shook his head, trying to make it stop. "She's sedated."

Tom reared back. "Sedated? What for?"

Gene explained what the doctor had said, including the fact that she shouldn't be alive.

Then he held up the pictures, letting them unroll.

His cousin's expression went from knitted brows to wide-eyed and slack-jawed. He even blinked.

Gene might've laughed if the situation was different.

"Dude. Didn't you think? Rule number one—always use protection?" Tom asked.

They'd made the rules after there was a time Gene had gotten an STD from a questionable girl at a bar in Casper, Wyoming, years ago.

He curled his lip. "Did *you* remember rule number one?" Gene snapped.

Tom's face flushed red. He snatched the pictures, not answering. "Looks just like you, a little monster."

"Excuse me?'

His cousin laughed. "What are you going to do? I guess, it could be pretty exciting. What did Jessica say?"

Gene snatched the paper back. "Nothing, Tommy. She said nothing. I found these in her hand after they sedated her. It must not be mine, so she was keeping it to herself." His voice cracked. He hoped his cousin hadn't caught that.

He'd never wanted kids, so why did it bother him so much that she was having someone else's kid?

"Hello, Gene," a sultry female voice spoke from behind them, startling them both.

Gene faced the woman, ready to fight. In the same heartbeat, he released the tension in his shoulders, let his arms fall to his sides, and let out a sigh.

It was the same Fayefolk they'd seen in the cave when Tom had been mortally wounded.

He stood in between the newcomer and his love's best friend. Jessica would kill him if anything happened to her bestie.

Tom joined him, putting a hand on his shoulder before turning to the Faye woman. "Who are you?"

"Please, call me Neeka. To answer your unspoken plea, I'm afraid I can't heal her."

"Why not?" Tom asked, his question soaked in desperation.

"Because there's nothing wrong with her." Neeka's expression was drawn; concerned and sad.

His cousin looked back and forth from Alex to Neeka. "Then why won't she wake up?" There was no mistaking the break in his voice.

It tore at Gene's heart.

"She's keeping herself trapped this way. Until she decides to let go, she'll remain like this."

Tom moved back over to the bed, his expression desperate for Alex.

Gene took a deep breath and made himself look away from his cousin's pain. "Neeka, can you help Jessica? She's in the other room."

"No, Gene. There's something at work in Jessica, that if I get involved in the outcome, it could have dangerous results," the Faye woman said.

"Is she going to be all right?" He needed some sort of reassurance.

"That's yet to be decided." Her voice had an ominous edge that made him frown, but her expression was sad again.

"What about her baby?" Gene cringed, debating whether he really wanted to know the answer.

Neeka's aquamarine eyes were intense. "*Your* baby's just fine right now."

He rubbed his hand over his face and back into his hair as he paced back toward the door away from the Faye, not letting her other words sink in.

"I can't stay," Neeka said. "Things are bad and I must return. The next few hours depend on the girls. Their strength will make all the difference. I ask that you protect them, Gene, like your life depends on it. For it does."

He whirled, ready to demand what she meant, but the Fayefolk was gone. He glanced at Tom.

They were both helpless.

All they could do was wait.

Alex

Alex was trapped. It was dark and cold. Her body moved, but not of her own free will. She could see and hear but not do anything to get out.

Now she was truly lost.

No light, no sound.

She'd tried to call Jessica, but her voice wouldn't work.

Fear paralyzed she.

Alex cried for Tom, but no sounds came out. There were moments when she heard his voice, and it sent a rush of warmth through her, but it quickly faded, reminding her of a mirage.

Am I dead? Is this hell?

There was nothing—just emptiness.

For a moment, she was convinced she felt Tom next to her, his gentle touch on her cheek.

"Jade, please come back to me," floated in the surrounding air like a whisper.

He'd called her Jade.

Alex's heart melted at hearing him use her first name.

"Jade, you can't leave me. I finally made it back to you. You can't do this to me."

The words seemed closer somehow. Heat warmed her as he spoke. This time, it lingered longer.

"Alex, come back." His voice was urgent; a demand.

She felt the warmth of his hand on her face.

Alex focused on the feeling.

She emitted a small whimper.

It was the first sound that reached her ears, unlike her earlier screams that never exited her mouth.

"That's it, Alex, come back to me! You can do it." Tom's voice was an encouraging plea.

Her hand twitched.

Alex fought to wake up, like wading through quicksand.

Tom wrapped his fingers around hers, squeezing them. Again, she could feel it, as if his touch was a lifeline.

He gave her something to lock them together and pull her back.

Tom's lips pressed against hers, and Alex felt power rush through her.

She clung to it desperately, wanting with all her heart for it to be Tom.

Her lips moved against his, and he kissed her gently.

She was afraid to stop, lest she fall back into her sleep. Her hand came up to touch his arm, by its own accord, and Tom finally pulled back.

"Tom," she whispered.

He wrapped her in his arms.

"Tom, I was so scared," Alex said into his shoulder.

"I know, baby. It's all right. You're safe now." He gently rocked her.

Alex enjoyed his embrace for several heartbeats. She was just grateful to be with him again.

They didn't speak, but maybe they didn't need to.

"Tom, what happened to me?" she asked finally.

He pulled back and their gazes met. "Judith possessed you."

"That would explain the lack of control. But how? You gave me this," she said, reaching up to touch her necklace.

"Jessica found it in the bathroom this morning. You must've forgotten to put it back on after your shower."

Alex struggled to remember. Her eyes teared up as she retraced her steps. "Is that what happens? You're forced to watch whatever they do with your body, then they throw you in a well?"

"You were in a well?" Tom asked.

"I don't know. It was dark and cold. And I couldn't move or yell out. Then I heard you. You called me, and I tried to find you. Then you were kissing me, and I wished you would never stop."

He smiled and leaned in, kissing her again. The fire in the movement of their mouths chased the last of the cold from her.

CHAPTER
TEN

CHAPTER TEN

**Tom*

Alex leaned back in the bed and glanced around. "How long have I been here?"

"A few hours," Tom said, sitting on the very edge of the bed, holding her hand.

"It felt like an eternity," she said. "Oh no! Jessica, she's in the cellar."

"It's all right," he soothed. "She's down the hall. Her heart rate was erratic, so they sedated her to get her body to reset."

"Oh no! Is something wrong with the baby?" Alex tried to get up.

He wrapped his hands around her arms to stop her from getting up. "Calm down, everything's going to be fine." He squeezed her upper arms, so she'd meet his eyes. "Why didn't you tell me?" he asked. Hurt darted across his expression.

She searched his face. "I couldn't. It wasn't my secret to tell."

"Don't you trust me? It's okay if Jessica moved on."

"Of course I trust you," Alex cried. "I wanted to tell you, but I couldn't. I couldn't betray Jessica like that."

Tom stood and turned away, running a hand back through his hair. "Hunters don't get happy endings, Alex. It'd be better if you both moved on."

What was he saying?

He didn't want her?

Gene wouldn't stick around for his kid?

"If I'd told you, you would've told Gene, or even if you didn't tell him, you'd find a way to drag him back. But it had to be Jessica's choice to tell Gene she was carrying his child."

Tom faced her again, his mouth hanging open. "I heard what Neeka said, but it's a shock."

The words were a whisper Alex barely heard. "Is it true? Is Gene really going to be a father?"

Alex nodded.

"Would that make me an uncle or like a second cousin, twice removed?"

That made her laugh. "I think you'd be a second cousin, but you two are like brothers, so I am sure uncle would make more sense."

Tom ran his hand over his face. "The ramifications are astounding. The Priest name will carry on. But so will the persecution." Again, his voice was so low, that Alex barely made out the words. He crossed back to the bed and sat in the chair next to her. "I wish you'd told me."

"I wanted to," she whispered. "Every day, I wanted to, but you know I couldn't force that on them."

"But we could've figured out a way to get them together, make them talk," Tom said.

"Oh, trust me. It crossed my mind, but she would never have done that to me." Alex watched Tom's jaw clench and unclench while he processed what she'd just said.

"Does that mean if you had gotten pregnant, you wouldn't have told me?"

"No, Tom. Of course, I would've told you. But Gene left without even saying goodbye. And he hasn't contacted her since."

"You're right." He looked down as if he couldn't meet her eyes. "I lied for Gene about the reason we left in such a hurry. So, I have no right to be upset at you for hiding this when I had lied first. But…"

Alex let out a breath. "She loves him, Tom. She doesn't want to admit it, but she does."

Tom smiled. "I'm gonna be an uncle."

Alex laughed. "Yes, you are."

*Gene

Gene left his cousin with Alex wrapped in his arms and returned to Jessica's room. He sat and grabbed her hand.

He frowned and stared into her face. She did look a little gray.

She slept in her still sedated state, and he couldn't look away.

She might die, her skin gray and cold, but she was still gorgeous.

Gene swallowed. He didn't want to think about the "d" word, no matter how many times he'd seen it, in his line of work.

He lifted the covers to slide his hands across to Jessica's belly. Hopefully, she wouldn't mind or think touching her was an invasion.

There was definitely a hard mound just under her waistline, a protective casing for a growing child.

He leaned forward so he could whisper to the little creature in her abdomen. "I don't know if you can hear me, little one, but you need to stay strong for your mother. I'm sure she loves you very much. I can't believe I'm your daddy but always remember this, too. Family isn't only blood. If you ever need anything or anyone, I will always be there for you."

The familiar prickling before his tears came, burned the corners of his eyes. He'd never wanted to be a father.

Family life wasn't for him. Hunters weren't meant to have a family.

Somehow, he couldn't wholly regret the child growing inside Jessica.

He held his right hand still on her bare skin, glancing at the pictures in his other hand. His eyes went blurry, he stared at the printout so hard. He blinked hard a few times to clear his vision. He had an overwhelming feeling of love for something he didn't even know yet.

Gene's hand grew warmer, heat radiating from where his skin met Jessica's. He studied her peaceful, beautiful face.

Her cheeks pinked while he watched as if she was flushing the gray away with a switch.

Gene hit the call button.

She appeared shortly, and checked Jessica's vitals, then went out to call the doctor.

When the doctor came in, he rechecked the vitals before speaking. "She's doing better. This is what we were hoping for. The sedation has given her body a chance to reset and her color has come back."

Gene didn't want to tell the doctor all *that'd* happened in the last few minutes. He'd seen enough miraculous things in his life and he didn't want to jinx this one, nor did he want to have to explain any of it to the doctor. "So we can wake her up now." It was more of a statement than a question.

"She'll wake up soon. We're relieved she's improved so quickly."

He glanced at his watch. Jessica had been out for about an hour and a half, so it could be a while longer. He didn't want to wait. He wanted to talk to her now.

Gene needed to tell her he didn't care that she was pregnant, that he still wanted to be with her.

When the doctor left, he pulled the chair closer, next to her bed, his head resting in his hands.

"Gene?"

He sat up. He must've dozed off.

She was looking at him, sitting up in her bed.

"Hey, how are you feeling?" he asked.

"You're still here," Jessica whispered.

"Of course, I'm still here." He moved to sit on the bed. He looked at the rolled-up paper in his hand. "I want you to know I understand," Gene said without meeting her gaze, instead looking down at his hands.

Her eyes were tear-filled when he mustered the balls to look at her again.

His jaw worked as he searched for words. "I've been miserable the last few months without you, but I know that you've moved on. I just want you to know that if you ever need anything, I will be here for you."

"What'e you talking about?" Jessica frowned.

"I found this in your hand," he admitted, handing the little printout over.

She touched his fingers and gently pulled at the ultrasound paper. "It's a relief that you know. Now I can stop worrying about whether or not I should tell you. I'm sorry, Gene," Jessica said, pushing herself up to a sitting position. "I didn't want you to find out like this, but that's what had happened, I guess."

"And it's mine." He said it as a statement, but she heard him wrong.

Jessica frowned, and anger shot across her pretty face. "How can you ask me if it's yours?"

"I- it's- that's not what-"

She quickly interrupted him. "So you think I started sleeping around as soon as you left? And got knocked up by some redneck hick?" She reached back and released her hand before he could move.

A burst of pain shot into his cheek. Gene's head turned with the impact. He stood up, backing away from the bed. "What the hell? I'm trying to tell you I missed you and you slap me?"

"What kind of slut do you think I am, Gene?"

"I didn't say you were a slut."

"But you implied it. You implied that I *'got myself in trouble'* with some random guy," she snapped, using finger quotes.

"That's not what I meant. I was saying, it's mine. Not questioning it. But why didn't you tell me?" He took a deep breath so he wouldn't give in to the anger stirring in his own gut.

"Did it ever occur to you I didn't tell you because you left without a word? Without a phone call?" Jessica asked. Her hands formed tight fists. "Why should I let you be a part of the greatest thing in my life when you didn't want to be with me in the first place?" Tears streamed down her face.

"I left to protect you," Gene shouted back.

"Protect me? What the hell is that supposed to mean?"

"You don't know the things we hunt. Do you think the Wendigo was scary? That ain't the half of it. And all those things are after Tom and me; they'd come for you, too. Do you think I want that? You think I want you to get hurt because of me?"

"But you *did* hurt me, Gene. You. All by yourself. Not one of your monsters, *you.*"

The lights began to sizzle and flicker as their tempers flared.

"You were the one that walked away, and if that wasn't bad enough, you took Tom away from Alex. She was devastated. She barely spoke for a week. And just when things were finally getting back to normal, I found out I was pregnant!"

The overhead light made a loud popping sound, as the long fluorescent bulbs exploded.

Gene jumped away from the shower of glass.

"Hey! What's going on in here?" Tom stuck his head in the doorway. "We could hear you arguing from down the hall!" He looked at Gene. "Why's it dark in here?"

"The light bulbs blew out," he said, glancing at Jessica, who was still visibly fuming.

"Well, I can hear you in Alex's room. Do you need a referee?" Tom asked.

"No. We need maintenance. Besides, we were just discussing why Jessica didn't feel I deserved to know I was going to be a father," Gene barked, gesturing at Jessica.

"You didn't," his cousin said simply.

Gene threw him a glare, half-angry, half-shocked. How dare Tom not be on his side?

"You walked away, man. You wanted her to live her life, and she has. If you want to be a part of it now, I suggest you apologize and let *Jessica* decide what's best for her and her child." Tom looked from Gene to Jessica and back again. "I'm going back to Alex. You two figure this out." He closed the door behind him.

Gene stared at the door. What the hell was he supposed to say?

He was never one to apologize, especially when he'd thought he was doing right by her— but now the game had changed.

Gene opened the hospital room door all the way again, to bring in the light from the hall.

"Gene?" Jessica's voice was tentative.

When he glanced at her, Jessica's hands rested on her belly.

She reached a hand to him.

He sat next to her again.

"I'm glad you know now. And I want you to be part of our child's life, but I need to know if you even want to be," she said. She was quiet and nervous.

Gene reached for her belly. He hesitated until she moved her other hand out of his way, then rested a warm his fingers on the slight bump. He looked up into Jessica's eyes and took a deep breath. "I love you, Jessica. And I want to protect you both. I don't know if I can, but I will do everything in my power to have this child with you."

Jessica smiled and leaned forward, pressing her lips to his.

CHAPTER
ELEVEN

CHAPTER ELEVEN

*Jessica

Jessica understood why the doctors wanted to keep them overnight for observation, but she really wanted answers.

Gene had told her how they'd said her blood work had some anomalies, but when they came and took more vials to retest, the nurse said everything was normal, and they must have read the tests wrong.

She was more than ready to get out of there, so she didn't argue. However, it was something she tucked away to bring back up later.

When they released her and Alex, it was a chilly morning, so Tom waited with them just inside the hospital doors, until Gene pulled up in the Mustang.

He came around to help Jessica in the car after his cousin climbed into the back with Alex. He reached over and held Jessica's hand as he drove.

She felt a sense of pride, knowing that he'd helped create the child growing inside her.

Jessica looked in the side mirror, catching Alex staring out the window and fingering the Guardian Spirit necklace Tom had given her.

"Are you all right?" Tom asked her best friend.

"I don't want to go back," Alex admitted.

"Why not?" Tom asked.

"Yeah, why not?" Jessica echoed.

"Judith tried to kill us."

"I don't think so," Tom said. "I think she knew those guys were coming, and she was trying to protect you."

"Regardless, she needs to be put down," Gene said.

"You can't just put her down like some rabid animal," Jessica said.

"Watch me," Gene said. "I just need to find her bones and salt and burn the bitch."

"She's my great-great-grandmother. She's not a bitch!" Jessica frowned, trying to keep reins on her temper. "She may have saved our lives." "Gene's right, unfortunately. We need to help her move on. If we hadn't come when we did, we might not have found you in time."

"Please, Jessica. I can't live there after what she did to me. I was... was..." Alex started hyperventilating.

Jessica reached back over the seat and grabbed her bestie's hand. "All right, we'll help her cross over." She turned back to Gene. "But I don't want you to destroy her."

"Fine. As long as she can't hurt our child," Gene said, grabbing her hand.

Jessica winced a little at how tight he squeezed.

The sheriff waiting for them when they pulled in. "Good to see you home safe."

"What brings you by this morning, Sheriff?" Gene asked.

"I wanted to let you know I caught those boys that busted up your place. Arrested them for attempted murder."

Gene frowned. "I thought they were just vandals."

"Well, it turns out they were drunk, again, when I caught up to them, and they admitted on video that 'they's gonna kill them Ferguson witches,' so they won't be going anywhere for a long time. Most folks around here appreciate you finding those kidnapped people, although I still don't know if I really understand what happened out there."

"Trust me, Sheriff, you don't wanna know," Tom said.

"Probably not." The older man smirked. "Well, I'd best get back to town. You girls let me know if there's anything you need."

Sheriff Wilson left, and she didn't miss the guys exchanging a look.

"Why don't you girls go in and rest while Tom and I look around and see if we can find out where Grandma's buried?" Gene suggested.

"I know where she is," Tom said.

All eyes landed on Tom.

"She's in the storm shelter, where she took the girls."

"Do you think she took them there just so she wouldn't be alone?" Gene asked.

"No, I don't think so. I think she was trying to protect them," he said.

Jessica glanced at the barn.

Judith was visible, standing by the door, clear as day.

Jessica headed toward the barn.

Gene and Tom followed.

Judith faded as they approached, but once she stepped into the barn, the ghost was by the open door to the storm shelter.

She was still transparent but at the same time, was somehow clearer.

They stood there in silence, looking at each other.

"What happened to you? Why are you still here?" she asked.

"I was trying to protect you, Edith. You're my baby, and I didn't even get to watch you grow up," the spectral said, her voice and demeanor sad.

"Judith, I'm not Edith. I'm Emily Jessica. Your great-great-granddaughter."

The ghost cocked to one side. "Not Edith?"

"Your daughter lived a good, long life, Grams. She got married and had two daughters, just like you. Edith died before I was born, though. I'm sure she's waiting for you on the other side." Jessica gasped when the apparition reached for her cheek. Instantly, her skin went cold. She could feel each digit as it touched her. "How?" she whispered. "How are you able to touch me and say more than two words? We've barely seen you the last few months."

Jessica felt the warm hand of Gene on her lower back. She knew he was giving her the silent support she needed. The sound of shoes on gravel let her know Tom was also there.

"I see you, Emily Jessica. You give me the strength I'd otherwise not have. You are of my line and are one step closer to discovering who you really are." Her translucent appearance flickered for a moment like she was a flashlight losing its battery power.

"I'm your great-great-granddaughter," Jessica repeated.

She already knew who she was, so what did Grams mean by that?

"Grams, what happened to you?" she pressed. She had to know.

Judith paced the length of the back of the barn.

Floating back and forth was more like it because her see-through feet didn't touch the dirt floor.

"George was down at the lake fishing, and it was getting late. I fed the children and got them off to bed; then, I went in search of George. I thought for sure he'd been in the moonshine again and lost his way back. I was piping mad, fixin' to give him a piece of my mind, when I saw this creature bending over something. It looked up at me with its yellow eyes and fangs dripping with blood. At first, I thought it was a wolf, but as it rose, it became bigger than a man. That's when I looked to see what it was eating, and it was my George." She paused, as if seeing the creature in front of her.

"How did you escape?" Jessica asked.

"I ran like the devil was chasing me. I hollered at Edith to get her sister and her cousin to the back storm shelter while I headed to the barn," Judith said.

"You hid in the shelter," Tom said, stepping closer to Jessica.

Judith looked at him, as if surprised to see him.

"Emily, you should've gotten married first. Then you wouldn't be in this predicament." Judith's gaze landed on Gene. "And you!" She pointed. "You best step up and take care of my girl. She needs a man who can take care of her and that baby you helped make."

Gene smirked, causing knots in Jessica's belly.

Her Grams was saying precisely what she'd wished she could.

"Don't you be acting all proud of yourself. Any fool can make a baby, but it takes a man to stick around and raise 'em," Judith said.

"Yes, ma'am. I intend to," Gene said.

"And you best be making an honest woman of her. Don't want folks talkin' bout my girl getting' herself in trouble."

Jessica frowned as Gene tried to appease the ghost without promising to marry her.

She] moved her focus back on the ghost, though. She didn't want Gene to salt and burn her if they didn't have to.

"I'm going to be all right. We're all good. It's time for you to rest now."

The ghost looked worried as any mother would.

"I just wanted to protect my babies, protect our line," she said.

"I know. But George is surely missing you. And I'm strong. I have Gene, Alex, and Tom. We'll be all right. Please, rest," Jessica said. Tears burned her eyes and one hot one rolled down her cheek. More would soon follow.

The ghost smiled. "You take care of your friends, too. They are your family."

"I will," Jessica promised.

Judith shimmered and faded.

Jessica turned toward the barn door.

Alex hovering just outside.

"She's gone," Jessica whispered, barely holding back a sob. She caught sight of Tom going to Alex.

Her best friend stepped into his arms.

When they left the barn and went into the old farmhouse, Tom took Alex upstairs, and Gene led Jessica to the kitchen.

Tom volunteered to tidy up the bedrooms quickly in the trashed house, just enough for the girls to take a nap.

Jessica was grateful because she didn't have the energy to deal with the mess.

Gene

Gene needed to put Judith to her final rest, but not while Jessica was around.

He took her inside and made her a sandwich. He sat with her while she ate, although she said nothing.

When she was finished, he took her upstairs for a bath.

He started the water as Jessica undressed. He stopped, stunned, as he saw her for the first time without clothes and a small baby bump showing on her belly.

She was incredibly sexy.

His body responded to the sight of her but now was not the time.

She was exhausted and still needed time to recover.

Somehow, the interaction with Judith had drained her again.

Gene helped her into the tub and kissed her gently. "Just relax for a while. Tom and I will go find a place where we can lay Judith to rest."

Her blue eyes were rimmed in red when she met his gaze.

"Behind the house, there's an enormous tree. There's a marker there for her husband. I wouldn't be surprised if they'd spent a lot of time by that tree together."

He smiled. "All right. Then that's where we shall put her."

"Thank you, Gene." Her smile was soft, but still watery.

"For what, sweetheart?"

"For coming back for me."

"I never should've left," he said, kissing her forehead. He had to force himself to leave. He didn't want to leave her alone, even if she was only relaxing in a warm bath.

His cousin was waiting at the top of the stairs when Gene came out of the bathroom. "Ready?" Gene nodded, and they headed outside.

"Where do you want to do it?" Tom asked.

He told his cousin about the big tree Jessica had mentioned.

"I'll get Grandma, you get the supplies," Tom said, heading for the barn.

An hour and a half later, they stood by the open grave.

Tom poured salt over the remains. "Are you sure you want to do this? Jessica will be pissed if she finds out."

"She can be as pissed as she wants, as long as she's safe." Gene lit the matches and dropped them in.

CHAPTER
TWELVE

CHAPTER TWELVE

*Alex

Alex sat straight up in bed. "Tom!" she cried, her breath coming in ragged gasps. She scanned the room, as tears poured down her face.

She couldn't focus on anything and her vision blurred from the waterworks.

It was like nothing had ever happened.

Had it all just been a nightmare?

Tom hadn't really been there. Her heart broke. It'd all been a dream.

Alex collapsed forward onto the bed, folding herself in half.

He's not here

Heavy footsteps pounded up the stairs. It must be Jessica.

Her head came off the purple comforter, and her heart jumped to her throat.

Tom rushed into the room, scooped her into arms, and pulled her close.

"You're really here. It wasn't just another dream," she sniffed.

"I'm here, Alex. I'm not going anywhere," Tom said, burying his face in her hair.

Alex pulled back, looked up into his eyes, and kissed him. Her kiss was desperate as she tugged his navy blue shirt off.

Tom complied as if he wanted her just as much.

She scooted back on the bed, and he kicked off his brown slip-on shoes and moved completely onto the mattress.

Alex pressed him down on his back, kissing him as she unbuckled his belt. She broke their kiss to pull off his pants and boxer briefs.

"Alex, are you sure?" She looked up at him, her stomach roiling with the fear of rejection.

"It's just that you were in the hospital and I don't want to wear you out."

"I need you, Tom, right now," she begged. She needed to *feel* him, know that he was real.

He leaned up and pulled her against him, lying back down with her stretched on top of him. His hands roamed over her body, still in her pajamas.

Alex's lips moved from his lips to his neck, then up to his ear.

Tom's groan of pleasure as her tongue explored his ear filled her with relief.

Alex pushed to her knees and pulled off her shirt before she resumed kissing her way down his sculpted body, her breasts gliding against him.

His body tensed as she kissed his hipbone, and he sucked in a breath.

She adjusted herself on the bed. She'd been wanting to do this for so long. Alex ran her tongue from the base of his cock to the tip.

A sound of pure pleasure escaped Tom's lips, his fingers tightening on her shoulder.

She swirled her tongue around his tip before wrapping her lips around him. She loved giving him pleasure.

Alex worked him up and down until he was practically writhing, then she hummed.

"Oh, Alex," Tom panted.

She worked him to the brink, tasting a little of him that he could no longer hold back. Then she quickly slipped off her shorts and panties and straddled him.

At first, she just ground against him, letting the moisture between them build, then she settled into place and plunged herself down on him.

They both groaned at the pleasure of being together again.

Alex rode him, her thighs squeezing him.

Tom bucked beneath her, keeping her rhythm.

They took their time, the pleasure building in both of them.

Alex's body spasmed around him, bringing him to join her.

He released himself into her, connecting them in a way she'd never thought possible.

Alex collapsed on top of him, completely spent.

He gently rubbed circles on her back as they both caught their breath. "So, I'm guessing you missed me?" Tom asked, smirking.

She looked up at him, flashing a coy smile. "Now, what would make you think that?"

He smiled and kissed her again. "I missed you too, baby."

She slid off to his right and rested her head on his chest. Alex's fingers traced over his tattoo.

They lay there quietly for a while.

Alex could feel Tom's breathing deepen as he dozed off. He was probably exhausted; he hadn't slept last night in the hospital.

She waited until he was fully asleep before she slipped out of bed for a shower.

Jessica

. . .

Jessica awoke with Gene spooned up behind her. His hand lay over her belly, fingers splayed protectively over their baby.

This is how it should always be.

She regretted having to get up when she was so comfortable with him, but nature was calling, so she slipped out of bed.

He woke when she moved as if primed for trouble. He was immediately tense. It filled her with a warmth, that he was so protective of her. And their baby.

"It's all right. I just have to go to the bathroom, go back to sleep," she whispered.

Gene smiled and settled back into the bed. "How long have we been asleep?"

Jessica glanced at the clock on her nightstand. "It's only one in the afternoon. We've only been in bed for two hours. I'll be right back."

She had every intention of returning to bed, and Gene's warm embrace, but her stomach had other plans, growling loudly, so she slipped downstairs for a snack.

She found Alex cooking in the kitchen. Her bestie stood there, barefoot, in her blue pajamas, covered with moons and stars. "I didn't know you were up."

"I was hungry and couldn't remember the last thing I had to eat. I thought I'd throw something in the crock pot for later while I fixed myself something quick to eat," Alex said.

"That's a good idea."

"How do chicken and dumplings sound? Easy crock pot meal."

Jessica put her hand on her belly. "I can't feel anything yet, but the baby says that sounds yummy."

They both gave a small laugh at that.

"So, how's Gene doing with all this?" Alex asked as her friend took a seat at the small cafe table.

"Surprisingly well, considering the way he had to find out," Jessica said.

"That's good. Hopefully, he'll stick around." Her best friend smiled, returning to the counter and the food she was preparing.

"I hope so, but I can't really make him. He's used to being on the road. He seems to think that if he and Tom stop hunting, the world will end."

"Well, all we can do is to be there for them," Alex said. "I'm just as discouraged as you are about how to help them. Keep them." Her expression darkened, like she was sad, too.

"I don't even think they have a home," Jessica said. "They just live out of their car."

"No, they have a place. They call it *the depot*." Alex set two sandwiches on the table.

"The depot? That's a strange name for a house"

Her bestie let out a chuckle, the first real laugh she'd heard in days. Beyond the giggle they'd just shared about her baby.

"Well, it's really an abandoned train depot with a basement." Alex shrugged, sitting to join her friend. "I don't know all the details, just that it's really not too far from here."

"Really? Where is it?"

"Esbon, Kansas."

Jessica pulled out her phone and typed in the name. Esbon, Kansas, was a few hours away. South and slightly east of their location. However, it was a surprisingly straight drive.

She'd hoped that they'd be closer than that so he could spend time with their child. Jessica ran a hand over her growing belly.

All this time, Gene and Tom had been not that far away— provided they'd been at their depot, and not on a case.

She picked up the sandwich Alex had made, thanking her quietly. They both ate in silence, as if they were both contemplating what would happen next.

Jessica helped Alex clean up, then headed back up to bed with Gene.

Even before all this had happened, Jessica had been feeling tired more often. She'd found herself sneaking regular little cat naps while Alex worked outside. She felt guilty hiding it from

Alex, but she hadn't wanted her friend to worry. It was normal pregnancy stuff.

Gene was still asleep on his back, so she crawled into bed and rested her head on his chest.

He shifted, pulling her against him. "That was a long trip to the bathroom," he teased.

"I went to get something to eat. She was hungry," Jessica traced, gently rubbing her tiny baby bump.

Her man chuckled. "I'm sure *he* was."

Jessica arched an eyebrow. "What makes you think the baby's a boy?"

"It's a Priest, isn't it?"

"And what if it is a girl?" Jessica snapped, frowning.

"I'd be okay with that, but Priests mostly have boys."

"Mostly?" She hadn't missed the note of sadness Gene was probably trying to hide.

"My dad only had a boy; his brother only had a boy. And their dad had two boys."

She could tell he was leaving something out. "Gene," she whispered, touching his thigh.

He let out a rough sigh. "And a daughter. My Aunt Helen." He wiped his hand over his face. It was clearly something that brought him great distress.

"So, it could be a girl," she whispered, trying to lighten the mood.

"I hope not. My aunt died when I was six."

"Oh, Gene, I'm sorry."

Gene pulled Jessica back down. "I'll tell you all about her. But not right now. Let me just hold you, and keep the two of you safe, while I can."

Alex

• • •

Alex contemplated going back to bed with Tom, but the idea of falling asleep scared her. She was afraid that next time, she wouldn't be able to pull out of the darkness. Her heart raced.

No, she had to get out of there and get some air.

She headed outside to check on the horses. They were in a pasture where she'd repaired the fence, so they'd been fine while she was away.

Alex refilled the water trough. She felt like a ride.

Being on horseback always helped her relax.

She saddled up Ellie and headed out to the lake.

Alex had ridden out there several times since the guys had left.

She'd even explored the cave again, trying to replay what'd happened with Tom.

Her mind flashed back to that day,

I had a migraine, so I laid down. Then, suddenly, I knew he was hurt. I was going to lose him. I rode so fast to get to him. How did I know where to go?

I just steered Ellie straight to the cave. Then I walked in the dark straight to him. How did I know where he was?

Was he calling me? Could I hear his cries of pain? No, I don't remember hearing him. I just knew where he was.

Alex gulped as she remembered his torn body.

So much blood; I have to stop the bleeding. Tom, don't leave me. God, please save him. I don't want to live without him. He saves people; please take me instead. I'm nothing.

She burst into tears again, coming back to the present.

Alex was glad she was far from the house. She hadn't told Jessica the truth, but she hadn't been happy since they'd moved, and now, after what happened, she couldn't stay there.

Where am I going to go?

She didn't know if she had enough money left to move anywhere else.

I need a job.

I could go back to Colorado.

Maybe I can get my old job back.

She would be alone.

Would Tom come with me? Probably not. He has a job to do.

Any way she looked at it, she was going to have to leave.

Jessica has Gene now, and they are going to have a family. They don't need me hanging around.

She wished Tom would go with her, then it wouldn't be so scary.

Does he feel the connection that I do? I always get a feeling when something's wrong with him. That one time, he'd dislocated his shoulder on a hunt, and I couldn't reach him for a couple of days.

She stopped and dismounted, dropping the reins of her horse.

I have to know.

Alex closed her eyes and spun in a circle with her arms outstretched, until she felt dizzy. She stumbled and fell to the ground, her eyes still closed.

As her head cleared, she had no idea which way she was facing. As she concentrated on Tom, it was even clearer; he was to her one o'clock.

She opened her eyes and looked around.

Sure enough, the house was behind her to her left. It was just like when he was in the cave; she just felt drawn to him.

Is it just me or does he feel it, too? He never mentioned it.

Alex remounted and turned her horse back towards home. She'd been gone for over an hour and didn't want Tom to wake up and find her gone. He had enough on his plate, without worrying about her.

CHAPTER
THIRTEEN

CHAPTER THIRTEEN

Tom

Tom came out of the house, right as Alex rode into the yard. He took in the dark circles under her eyes and the paleness of her skin. It worried him, but it was probably just a lingering effect from what she'd been through.

"Hi," he said, keeping it simple. He burned to interrogate her, but made himself hold the questions and curiosity back.

"Hi." Alex smiled, slipping off the horse's back and coming closer, reins in hand.

"Did you have a nice ride?"

"Yeah, it was good," she said, not giving him much to go on.

He stepped up to her and leaned down to kiss her.

Alex sighed with what sounded like contentment, as he pulled away.

"You had me worried when I woke up alone," he admitted.

"Sorry. I was hungry, so I made a sandwich. Then I was too restless to sleep, so I went for a short ride."

She's covering up for something.

Alex had been gone long enough for him to know that it'd been more than a *short* ride.

"I thought you'd still be sleeping. I didn't mean to worry you," she said curtly, turning and heading toward the barn.

Tom frowned.

Had he said something wrong?

He followed her to where she tied her horse next to the barn.

Alex unsaddled the mare, and visibly hesitated at the door.

He'd closed the storm shelter after retrieving Gram's bones, but Tom could see it still bothered her to go inside.

She stiffened her back, put on a brave face, and went inside. Alex returned with tools and brushed down the bay mare, avoiding making eye contact with him.

He didn't like the awkwardness between them. "It looks like we'll be sticking around for a while. I was thinking you could teach me about horses, and I could help you around the place."

She glanced over Ellie's back and met his gaze. "You're staying?"

He smiled. "Well, Gene's not going to leave Jessica anytime soon, so I guess you're stuck with us."

"But what about your work?" Alex said, her tone and expression unreadable.

Tom shrugged. "No cases right now. Maybe I can convince Gene to retire and let someone else handle it."

"But would you be happy just staying on the farm?" she asked, her voice laced with concern.

He cocked his head and rounded the horse to her side. "I'd be with you, wouldn't I?" Tom pulled her into his arms.

Alex smelled of horse and leather, with just a hint of her body wash.

"I was thinking since Gene and Jessica are having a baby, maybe we could have a little family of our own," he said, his heart racing at the idea. He pulled her into a hug, lifting her from her feet. "Can you picture it, Alex? We'd have the prettiest baby!"

Alex's smile seemed forced when he set her back down and looked into her pretty face.

"Can you please go check on dinner for me and see if Jessica and Gene are hungry? It should be done by now. I don't want it to be too dried out."

Tom smiled and gave her a quick kiss before heading into the house. He went straight to the kitchen and lifted the lid on the crock pot.

Chicken and dumplings steamed up at him.

Tom took a deep breath, and his stomach rumbled at the tease of the aroma. He replaced the lid and headed upstairs. He knocked on Jessica's door. "Rise and shine! Dinner's ready!" He planted his ear on the door.

Jessica gasped and Gene growled, "Dammit, Tommy!"

Tom smiled to himself and trotted down the stairs. He set the table and dished up food as Jessica and Gene came sleepily down the stairs.

"Somethin' smells good," his cousin said, coming into the dining room.

"Alex made it," Tom said, proudly.

The three of them sat down and started eating.

Tom kept an eye on the door, waiting for Alex.

Jessica kept distracting him with questions about their hunts and what they'd been up to.

Way too soon, they were done eating and Alex had never joined them.

"Can you guys handle the dishes? I want to go check on Alex."

"I don't know, Tommy. It's an enormous responsibility. You think we can handle that, Jessica?"

Jessica giggled. "Yeah, I think we can handle it."

Tom was focused on the door when Jessica touched his hand. "I'm sure she's fine. She's probably just not hungry. It's as simple as that. We'd ate sandwiches a bit ago."

He flashed her a half-hearted smile, then headed outside.

The horses were in the pasture, so he headed to the barn. He didn't see her, but he checked all the stalls and the loft.

Still, there was no sign of Alex.

Where has she gone?

Tom checked around the back, but he hadn't seen her go inside. Maybe she'd slipped upstairs while he was putting the food on the table and had fallen asleep.

He went back into the house.

"Did you find her?" Gene asked, coming out of the kitchen.

"No," Tom said, not waiting for his cousin's answer. He just jogged upstairs. He checked her room and the bathroom, even the other two bedrooms, but no Alex.

Where could she have gone?

Gene and Jessica were settling into the sofa to watch a movie.

"Jessica, do you know where Alex might've gone?" Tom asked.

"Gone? Why would she have gone somewhere? Is her truck still here?" she asked, sitting up straighter.

"Her truck is here, and the horses are here, but I can't find *her.*"

"What happened?" his cousin asked. "Did you two have a fight?"

"No!" Tom shook his head. "We were talking in the barn and she asked me to get dinner dished out while she put Ellie away."

"*What* were you talking about?" Jessica arched a fine delicate eyebrow.

"Nothing bad. I asked her to teach me about horses," Tom said.

"And?" Jessica prompted.

"And? I may have mentioned that since you and Gene were expecting that maybe someday she and I could have a family," he confessed, a little embarrassed to admit it in front of his cousin.

The color drained from Jessica's face, sending waves of fear through Tom.

"Is her pack gone?" She pushed up from the couch.

"Her pack?" Tom asked.

"Yeah, she's got a survival bag in the horse trailer. It's one of those camping backpacks. She packed it not too long after y'all left. Alex said she didn't want to be unprepared in case of an emergency like that again. If the bag is gone, so is she. I'm just surprised she didn't take a horse," Jessica said, her voice not hiding obvious deep concern.

"Well then, she can't have gotten far," his cousin said.

"I wouldn't count on that," Jessica said. "Alex can move fast when she wants to. I'd head for the lake, though. She seems to find it serene there. But Tom, if she doesn't want to be found, you won't find her. Might be better to wait for her to come back."

"But why would she leave?" Tom asked, shaking his head and wracking his brain.

Had he done something wrong?

He was a hunter, so he didn't usually panic.

Right now?

Panic was eating him alive, like a snake weaving in and out of his guts, constricting as it slunk along.

"You'll have to talk to her. It's not my place to say anything, but if you want to go look for her, take a horse and pack with you. It'll get dark soon," Jessica said. "I'd go with you, but…"

Gene had what looked like a death grip on Jessica's arm. His cousin pulled the dark-haired beauty back to a sitting position.

"Find her, quick," his cousin said gruffly. "I don't think I can keep Jessica sitting here for long, not knowing where Alex is."

Tom nodded and headed out.

He saddled Anduril—the gelding he'd ridden before—and attached his saddle bags. They were packed with survival stuff as well, but what could one expect from a former forest ranger like Alex?

As he headed out toward the lake, he replayed their conversation, trying to figure out why she'd take off.

He couldn't put his finger on it.

Tom had thought things were great with them.

She wanted to be with him. She'd showed that today.

It'd been so hot with her, and it'd felt so right.

Was she afraid he'd leave again?

Had he said something to offend her?

As he rode, Tom scanned the area for her, but Jessica was right, if she didn't want to be found he wouldn't find her, unless...

CHAPTER
FOURTEEN

CHAPTER FOURTEEN

**Tom*

Tom rode straight toward her. Once he'd gotten a fix on Alex, he didn't have to slow down. He could feel where she was, like an invisible beacon, and if he kept following it, he'd find her. There was no doubt.

He stopped Anduril in front of the Wendigo's cave. His heart raced.

Something's wrong with Alex, but what?

To find her in the cave the Wendigo had been; he couldn't imagine why Alex would want to be in there.

He was concerned it was a situation like the guys who'd trashed her house. There were more misunderstanding citizens, blaming the girls for the Wendigo.

Perhaps they'd dragged her back to the scene of the crime, to torture her.

Tom could feel that she was in pain, and it'd made him push the horse to a dead run around the lake.

Anduril was covered in sweat as he sprang from his wide back.

Tom drew the demon blade he always carried even before he went into the cave. It would kill a human as quickly as a demon, and although he didn't want to have to kill anyone, he'd protect Alex with his life if need be.

Tom crept into the cave, shining his light around. He moved silently, trying to get the drop on whoever had taken her.

When he heard sniffling, he quickly switched off his light. There was a faint glow from a lantern ahead, so he made his way toward it. He paused when he heard her voice.

"Please, God, why couldn't you have taken my life for him that day? I was ready to die for him, but I can't do this to Tom. It's not fair."

Alex was praying.

He listened a moment longer.

She paused in her praying, like she was listening for an answer. Then she continued. "Faye? Can you hear me? If you can hear me, can you please tell me why it didn't end here? I was ready for that, but not this."

His heart was breaking for her, hearing her pray to more than one entity. The twisting inside him was almost more than he could bear.

Tom headed toward the lantern.

She was sitting next it, her knees folded up in front of her, her arms wrapped around them, and rocking slightly. Alex was facing the wall where the Wendigo had thrown him.

There was still blood spatter there—his blood.

"Alex?" he breathed.

She spun to face him, landing on her hands and knees. "Tom, how did you find me?" Alex backed closer to the wall.

"Are you alone?" He glanced around in the dark cave.

"Yes," she said.

Tom slid the blade back into the sheath and closed the distance between them. He knelt next to her. "Honey, what're you doing here?"

"I can't do this to you," she cried, sitting back on top of her feet.

"Do what? Baby, what're you talking about?" He reached for her. She scooted away.

"Alex, please talk to me."

The look on her face broke his heart.

"You deserve better than me," Alex sobbed. Her slender shoulders shook.

Tom tried to wait patiently for her to continue.

"It wasn't supposed to be like this. I was supposed to trade places with you."

"You're not making sense, honey."

"You were going to die. I couldn't let that happen. I prayed they would take me instead because you still had work to do here. But then the Faye... she... she healed you, and... And... I fell in love with you."

Tom took her hand.

This time, she didn't fight him.

"But I can't give you what you want," Alex said, not responding to his touch, but not pulling away either.

"All I want is you."

"No," she said, shaking her head. "You want a family. You deserve a family."

Tom cocked his head to one side. This was the reason she ran? "Alex, I want to have that family with you."

"I can't!" she cried. "I'm broken, Tom. I can't have children."

His heart raced, but he couldn't tear his eyes away. He took a moment to swallow. "I don't understand."

"I had an ovary removed when I was a teenager," Alex said, pulling up her shirt and pointing at the faint scar on her abdomen.

"But you have two, right? So, you still have another one?" Tom asked.

She shook her head. "The doctors said it would be highly unlikely that I'd ever have children because of the drop in my hormones."

The emotional pain that rippled across her face echoed within his own body.

Tom couldn't understand how she could be so distraught over an offhand comment he'd made about wanting to settle down with her.

He stroked her face.

"Do you know how hard it's been to watch Jessica for the last few months? And I couldn't even talk to you about it, and, well, I couldn't make Jessica feel bad because I can't have kids."

Tom might never be a father like Gene, but as he looked at Alex and saw how torn up she was about not feeling worthy, it hit him even harder.

It was *her* he wanted.

He'd never even considered becoming a parent until yesterday.

No, he and Alex could be happy here raising horses and working on a farm.

He curled his fingers to motion for her to come over to him.

She moved hesitantly into his embrace.

Tom sat in the dirt with Alex in his lap. He held her tight as if he could squeeze together the broken pieces of her heart. "We don't have to have kids to be happy," he whispered.

She looked up at him in the dim light. "But I want to give you everything," she said, staring into his face.

"You already have. You saved my life."

Alex frowned. "No, the Fayefolk did that."

"No, it was you. I've seen the Faye since then. Neeka is her name. And she said that she wouldn't have been able to heal me alone. You heard her that night, as did I. She said she heard your call through her kin. But when she touched you, it was like you drew her power and magnified it to heal me. Your eyes lit up like sunshine that night."

"But, Tom. She didn't touch me. Jessica was the only one who was touching me. That woman had her hand on Jessica."

"I don't really know what happened. But after everything I've seen in my life, I've learned not to take anything good for granted." He smiled to reassure her.

Alex still had doubt written across her face.

Tom let out a frustrated breath. "Besides, that wasn't even what I meant. You give me something worth living for. If we can't have kids, that's all right. We'll make the best aunt and uncle to Gene and Jessica's kids. And the best part is, we can spoil them rotten and give them back," he teased.

That made Alex smile.

"I know I haven't said this enough, but I love you. I haven't stopped thinking about you since the day we met," Tom confessed.

"Really?" Alex's voice was soft, doubtful.

He tried not to be offended by that doubt. "Of course! I've been plotting how to get back to my sunshine since the moment I left."

She looked down at his hand in hers, resting in her lap. "I can't stay here, Tom," she blurted, as if she was ripping off a bandaid.

"What?" He reared back. "I thought you liked it here."

"No, not really," she confessed.

"But you seemed so happy on the phone."

She looked up at him guiltily.

"Alex, why would you lie?" he asked, hurt churning in his gut.

"I wasn't sure I'd ever see you again. I didn't want you to feel guilty for leaving when you had no choice."

"Alex, when we left—"

"I know, Tom. There was no case. Gene was scared," she said, letting him off the hook.

"I shouldn't have gone with him."

"You had to! He's family."

Tom couldn't believe she was so understanding about it. Now it was his turn to do it for her. "So where should we go?"

"We?" Alex sounded leery, but a little hopeful, too.

"Did you think I'd just let you leave and not follow?" he asked, waggling his eyebrows.

"I really didn't think you'd want to be with me after you found out," Alex admitted.

Tom hugged her tight. "I love you, Jade Alexandria, and want to be with you. I don't care where we go. I've been on the road for so long now, and Gene's here to take care of Jessica. He's going to have his hands full with the new baby. So, if you want to leave, I'm happy to oblige. Don't worry, we can visit."

Alex threw her arms around his neck so fiercely it knocked him backward, where they lay in the dirt.

She cried into his shoulder. "I'm so relieved that you didn't reject me. In fact, you offered to go with me. I couldn't ask for more! I love you, too!"

Tom laughed as he held her.

Jessica

Jessica and Gene finished their movie, and he turned off the television.

"Do you think he found her?" she asked, putting her hand on her stomach and trying to ignore the knots from the unknown.

"He won't stop till he does. Tommy's like a dog with a bone when it comes to Alex. So why did she leave?"

"Oh, it's nothing."

"It can't be *nothing*, or she wouldn't have left."

"Sometimes she just needs to be alone," Jessica said.

He smirked. "Well, the way she and Tommy were going at it this afternoon, I doubt she wanted time away from him."

"Gene Priest! Were you eavesdropping on them?" Her face went hot.

Gene laughed. "No, ma'am. I was just getting out of the

shower and coming to curl up with you, and this house is old. Sounds carry." He shrugged.

"Better not have been," Jessica said, frowning.

"So, tell me what's really going on. I doubt you want me asking Alex," he said, his tone about as serious as she'd ever heard.

Jessica huffed, crossing her arms over her tender breasts.

He was right. She didn't want him to ask Alex, and if Tom found Alex, she'd tell him. So, Gene would eventually ask his cousin, anyway.

She ran a hand over her growing belly, looking down at the small bump there. "Alex can't have kids," she mumbled.

"Tom never wanted kids. Neither of us did. It's not the life we'd want for our sons," Gene said standing up, rubbing his hands on his thighs.

"Or daughters," Jessica said, again irritated he wouldn't think about the possibility their child could be a girl. "Well, Tom must've changed his mind because she wouldn't have left if he hadn't mentioned it."

"Neither of us thought children would *ever* be possible. Our fathers had been adamant about us 'being safe.' Tom and I had both decided long ago that no child deserved to be brought into a world so full of evil, so it never occurred to me that with you carrying my child, Tom may consider having a family, too. But really, he won't care. I'm pretty sure he's in love with Alex, so he'll still want to be with her either way."

"Alex won't see it that way," she said sadly.

"What d'ya mean?" Gene lifted his chin.

"If Alex thinks he wants a family, then she'll stay away from him until he moves on."

"That might never happen. I don't want to be too far from you and Tom, and we've always stuck pretty close together, so she's stuck with him," he said, as if that solved it. He reached a hand to her and pulled her up from the couch. "I know you're tired; I can see it in the drooping of your eyes. Let's get you upstairs."

"I don't think I can sleep, not knowing if she's okay." Jessica started crying. "I'm sorry," she whispered while wiping away the tears.

"It's all right, baby. Tom will find her."

"It's not just Alex. It's everything. I'm—" she hiccupped.

"I know," Gene whispered.

"You don't know! I'm glad you're here, but ... I'm... I'm... overwhelmed. These stupid hormones! I'm worried about Alex. I'm afraid for our baby. And I'm still freaking out about the damage those assholes did to my house! I don't know how to make all these emotions go away!"

He wrapped her in his arms and held her close. "I'm here now and I'll do whatever I can to help you. Let's take it one step at a time. Starting with heading upstairs."

Jessica allowed him to lead her upstairs.

It wasn't really that late, but he let her know, with just one lustful look, that sleep wasn't what he intended.

She was okay with that.

Tom

Tom dropped an armful of branches next to the small fire that Alex had started. He had convinced her to move out of the cave because he didn't want the reminder of what the Wendigo had done to him.

They were on the small beach of the lake, near the cave, but at least it was out of sight, and that was as good as he could hope for right now.

He squatted down and fed a few of the branches to the small flame.

Alex sat staring into the fire.

He moved over to sit next to her on the sleeping mat she'd unrolled to sit on.

The sleeping bag she'd been wrapped in while in the cave was sitting in a pile next to her.

"You meant it, didn't you?" she asked finally.

Tom didn't need to ask what she referred to. He smiled. "Of course. Although, I'm not sure why you want to leave."

"Jessica and Gene will need some time to build their family, and they don't need me hanging around being the third wheel."

"I wouldn't leave you here with them to be the third wheel," he said.

"And the more I'm around her, the more I want a child that I'll never have. I just need to get away for a while." A silent tear slid down Alex's cheek.

"Why don't you come to the depot with me for a while?" Tom asked.

She arched an eyebrow. "The depot? An underground bunker? After what Judith did? I don't think I could be trapped like that again."

He laughed. "Well, Gene likes to refer to it as the Bat Cave, but it's just our home. Come stay with me. It doesn't feel like we are 'trapped underground,' as you put it. It's cozy."

Alex gave him a hard, long look, saying nothing.

It was wrecking his insides.

"You can show Gene how to take care of the horses and we'll have a place to stay that's not too far away if they need us, but it's far enough away that you can have your break," Tom said, trying not to sound like he was begging.

"For how long though? I need to find a job, Tom. I'm running out of money. I've used up almost all of my savings."

"Money's not a problem, but for now, let's start with a week, and go from there. Think of it as a vacation before you start a new job. We even have internet there, so you can stay 'til you find something."

"Are you always going to be my knight in shining armor?" Alex teased.

Tom smiled. "If you'll let me."

CHAPTER
FIFTEEN

CHAPTER FIFTEEN

*Tom

Tom awoke in the morning and stretched out on the mat he and Alex had been sharing.

She'd unzipped the sleeping bag, and they'd curled up together under it last night.

Unfortunately, now he was alone. He sat up.

There was a pot sitting in the middle of the fire with something bubbling in it. His stomach growled, reminding him it'd been a long time since he'd eaten.

probably hadn't eaten last night at all. She'd left before dinner and had been so distraught when he'd found her.

Rustling sounds caught his attention, and Tom looked up.

Alex came out of the woods. "Good Morning!" She had a pronounced bounce in her step.

Her mood had definitely improved.

"Morning." He yawned and rubbed the sleep from his eyes.

"Did you sleep well?" she asked.

"Better than I thought, but not as good as in your bed." Tom smiled.

"Well, I do have a pretty nice mattress."

"You sure you don't want to stay and enjoy that good mattress?" He waggled his eyebrows.

Alex laughed. "You know, you could get a mattress like that one."

Tom lifted his chin. "I can't have it delivered to the depot and I'm not sure Gene would let me tie one to the top of his precious Mustang."

"I have a truck."

"Yeah, but then Gene would have to come help me move it."

"Really?" Alex asked, putting her hands on her hips.

"What?"

"Do you not want my help because I'm a girl?" She arched an accusing eyebrow.

"Not at all, but a mattress is big."

"What are you getting, a California King?" Alex smirked.

"No, but even queen mattresses are heavy."

She shook her head. "Jessica and I carried both of our new mattresses upstairs," she said. "Without a big man to help."

Tom smirked. "Well then, I guess we'll have to pick up a mattress on the way there."

She squatted by the fire across from him and stirred the pot.

"What's that?" he asked.

"Oatmeal. We should eat before we head back. It's a long walk."

"Oh, we don't have to walk..." Tom glanced around, panic inching up from his gut. In his worry for Alex, he hadn't tied Anduril. "Crap!"

"What?" Alex asked, her dark eyes going wide.

"I rode Anduril here, but I didn't tie him, so he probably went home without us."

"Wait, you rode him here?"

"Yeah, but I was trying to find you, and when I found out you were in the cave, I just forgot about him."

Alex stood up and whistled twice.

A whinny from a distance.

She smiled and knelt back down, serving Tom a bowl of oatmeal.

He wasn't usually an oatmeal eater, but he was hungry, so it was about the best thing he'd ever tasted.

"Tom, what did you mean when you said you knew I was in the cave?"

He cocked his head to one side. How honest should he be? "Don't you feel it, too?" he asked. "Ever since you healed me, I can just kinda sense where you are."

"You can?" she asked, blinking.

"It's more than that, though. I knew you were in trouble the night you were possessed. I just had this feeling you needed me, and I made Gene head back." He stared into her eyes. "Don't you feel the connection?"

An overwhelming fear vibrated through Tom.

What if she didn't feel it, or understood?

Would it scare her away?

What if she thought he was crazy or some stalker?

Alex stirred the oatmeal in her bowl like she was trying to find the words. "It was before that," she said, still avoiding his gaze.

"Before what?" Tom asked.

"The day you went to hunt the Wendigo. I got a nasty headache."

"Yeah, Jessica told us you had a migraine when she caught up to us."

"I went to lie down and fell asleep. I dreamed you were hurt… dying. I woke up and went out for you. I knew it wasn't a dream. It was real, and you needed me. I prayed all the way there that I'd get to you in time. I jumped on Ellie and rode to the meadow where I'd dropped you off, hoping to find clues to where you'd gone, but I rode straight to you. I didn't have to figure it out. I just *knew*. Even in the cave, I walked straight to you."

Tom nodded. "How is this happening? I've seen so many unusual things in my life, but nothing like this."

"I don't know. But ever since then, I always know where you are. Well, not specifically, but I know I can find you if you need me." Alex's face flushed an appealing pink.

"That's how I found you last night. I just followed my instincts, and they led to you."

Anduril came trotting into camp, interrupting their conversation.

"He came back?" Tom scrambled to his feet.

"Of course. He only wandered off to eat and apparently rolled in the dirt," she said, gesturing to the dirty, twisted saddle.

"Do all horses come when you call?" he asked.

"Well, not all of them, but I trained mine to do that," she said, as she unfastened and righted the saddle.

"You'll have to teach me how."

"Bribery." Alex smiled, reaching for Anduril's reins.

She finished her tasks with the gelding, then Tom helped clean up their little camp.

It didn't take long until they were on their way back to the house.

Alex rode behind Tom with her arms wrapped around him.

He had a feeling she hadn't slept at all, despite being wrapped in his arms.

She had her head against his back. Her hands that'd held him tight relaxed and slid from his waist as she dozed off.

He felt her slipping to the left. "Alex!" he cried, reaching with a quick arm to catch her.

She jerked awake and straightened on her own. "Sorry, I must've drifted off. I guess you calmed me more than I thought."

"Alex, did you sleep at all last night?"

"Um, a little." She sounded sheepish.

Tom could hear the lie in her voice. "When we get back to the house, I'm putting you to bed."

"Really? And will you spank me if I don't go?" she teased.

He smirked, but his cheeks burned. He wasn't really into that kind of thing, and she wasn't either, but the implication was hot enough. "If I have to." He tried to make it sound like a warning.

Alex giggled. "Tom Priest! I'd never have suspected!" She pretended to be shocked, but they both laughed.

Gene was on the porch when Tom and Alex rode into the yard.

"You're back! Good, I need you to run an errand with me," his cousin said.

"What kind of errand?" Tom asked, arching an eyebrow.

"One that will help the girls sleep better at night," Gene said, nodding toward the house.

"All right. Suits?"

"Yeah, I'm thinking so." His cousin stepped closer to the horse. "The damage to the house and the reminder that they came here to kill them is really stressing Jessica out. I think she's worried they might try again. So, you and I are going to put the fear of God in those boys and ensure that they never bothered our women from this day forward."

"Great idea. Just give me a few minutes," Tom said.

Gene threw him a nod and headed back inside.

Alex slipped down from behind Tom and took the reins.

He jumped down and followed her to the barn.

"What're you doing? I thought you had to go," she said, her eyes betraying her confusion.

"I do, but it can wait."

"Don't hurt those boys," she said sadly.

"I don't plan on it. That's why we wear the suits. It makes them afraid without having to get physical."

"All right, because they're just stupid guys. It's not worth it."

Tom's anger spiked from his gut. "They're not just *stupid guys!*"

Alex's face shot up, her brows knitted.

"Alex, they could've killed you both. They intended to. We can't just let that go. If those guys get out, what's to stop them from trying again?"

"I don't think they'll try again."

"What makes you think that?" Tom demanded.

"Because they're just drunk rednecks that got burned and didn't want to be embarrassed in front of their friends. After they spend some time in jail, they won't want to try again."

"Did you see what they painted on the wall?" he said, trying not to give into his exasperation. "They think you're a witch."

"Maybe they're right," Alex said, quietly slipping the saddle off Anduril.

Tom stared as she walked away to hang up the saddle. "What do you mean?"

She sighed. "I can't explain what happened in that cave. What if it *was* witchcraft?"

"You're not a witch. I've dealt with my share of witches, and you are definitely not a witch. It all comes back to the Fayefolk, Neeka. She's the one we need to get answers from. But not today." Tom put his arms around her. "Look," he said a little calmer. "Gene and I are just going to go let those jerks know we won't tolerate you being treated like this."

"Can you keep Gene's temper in check as well?"

"I'll do my best,"

Since Gene learned of the baby, he'd be even harder to rein in. However, Tom could do it. He'd do what he needed to. Like always.

"Just don't do anything stupid. Remember, I don't have bail money." Alex smirked.

"I won't. Promise," he said, leaning in and kissing her.

"Now go shower. You smell like a horse."

Tom laughed and headed into the house, with a quiet dare for her to join him.

CHAPTER
SIXTEEN

CHAPTER SIXTEEN

Gene

The sheriff looked at Gene and Tom with raised bushy eyebrows when they flashed FBI badges. "What can I do for you boys today," the older man inquired.

"Well, you asked us to watch out for those girls and we just want to make sure those boys understand what the consequences are for going on a witch hunt and threatening them," Gene said.

The sheriff smiled slowly. "Deputy Barnes, will you please take these special agents to an interrogation room?"

Tom followed his cousin down the hall and into the small room. "How do you wanna do this?"

"Oh, I think this is personal," Gene said.

He smiled. "That's what I was hoping you would say."

The two men were brought in and seated side by side at the table. Although they were handcuffed, the deputy didn't attach them to the table.

"Jack Jameson," he nodded at the man on the right, "Bill

Dredge," he indicated the other man. "They're all yours." The deputy left the room, the door slamming hard with his departure.

Tom stood casually under the camera, holding a device that looked like a small cellphone.

Gene glanced at him, and his cousin nodded. "You got it?"

"Yup." He waved the device.

Gene turned back to the guys at the table and flashed his badge.

"What the hell does the FBI want with us?" Bill spat.

"We want to know what would make you think that the girls living at the Ferguson farm are witches?" he asked calmly.

"What'd you care?" Bill continued.

"Just answer the question," he ordered, leaning on the desk, intentionally menacingly.

"They are witches. They wear pentagrams and the short one put a curse on me," Jack pointed out.

"What do you mean she put a curse on you?" Tom asked, still leaning back beneath the camera.

"She broke my nose, then when she was walking away she muttered a curse and now I can't—" He looked away, his face bright red.

"Can't what?" Gene asked.

"I can't get it up," he said, slamming his handcuffed hands down on the table.

Gene burst out laughing and turned to Tom. "Ya hear that, Tommy, they're blaming our dear little Alex for his impotence."

"Well, I guess he'd have to blame someone. No guy wants to admit that karma is preventing him from raping innocent women."

"She's not innocent! She wears the mark of the devil," Jack added, jumping to his feet.

Gene calmly removed his jacket and hung it on the chair on his side of the table. He loosened his tie and slipped it off. "Not innocent, huh?" he asked as if he didn't have a care in the world. He unbuttoned his sleeves and rolled them up before reaching for the top button on his shirt. "You might want to sit back down, sir."

"Those witches are the reason Shelley is dead!" Jack yelled, returning to his seat. "They brought some monster with them or conjured it, and now my girl is dead."

"That necklace look anything like this?" Gene asked, pulling the collar of his shirt to the side, revealing his tattoo.

The guys both pushed back from the table, their chairs making a horrendous scratching sound.

Tom set the device down on the windowsill, priming for trouble.

Gene leaned forward on the table. "Those girls had nothing to do with that thing. It was here long before they were. We rescued what victims we could, and those girls almost died in the process. Now, I wanna show you what happens to backwoods hicks that mess with my girl."

"You can't do anything to hurt us," Bill said cockily. "It'd all be on camera." He gestured to the equipment in the upper corner.

Gene smiled devilishly and pointed at the little black box on the window seal. "Ya see that little thing? It's a scrambler. Now, there's no evidence that you boys have even been in this room at all, thanks to that little baby."

The first dude bolted for the door, but Gene caught him and slammed his head to the wall.

"Now, now, leaving so soon?" he drawled, trying not to reveal his anger.

"We'll sue you," the other jackass said, standing again to defend his friend.

Gene grinned when his cousin's hand closed around the smaller man's throat.

Tom knew exactly how much pressure it took to render the man unconscious. He also knew how to snap the man's neck.

The guy's hands closed around Tom's wrists, but it didn't help.

At six foot five inches, his cousin was much larger than his opponent.

The man struggled as Tom squeezed hard enough to make it difficult for him to breathe, but not impossible.

"You touch my girl again, and you won't have to worry about going to jail. I have a shotgun and a shovel. I doubt you will be missed," his cousin growled and released his grip.

The loser collapsed to the floor, gasping for air.

The first one struggled with Gene to get free, but he had his arm twisted behind his back and his face pressed against the door.

"Now, I can tell that you boys are gonna start trying to use the brain between your ears rather than the one between your legs to do your thinking. Because if you don't, we know several places that your body would never be found."

The man whimpered.

"That's more like it," Gene growled and released the guy.

He backed into the corner away from Gene.

Gene looked at his cousin and nodded.

Tom picked up the device and they left the room.

The sheriff stepped out of the observation room as they closed the door to interrogation. "Nicely done, fellas," Sheriff Wilson said, holding out a hand.

They exchanged a look, then Gene shook the sheriff's hand.

"Wish I coulda done that. Those boys are nothin' but trouble," the older man said.

"We're going to do everything in our power to protect those girls," Tom said.

"Good. They deserve some honorable men to take care of them."

"We'll do our best, Sheriff," Gene said, and they headed for the car.

Jessica

. . .

Jessica was cleaning up the mess the vandals had left when Alex joined her.

They moved into the library, putting broken items in a large garbage bag.

"Everything all right?" Jessica asked.

"Yeah."

"Did you tell Tom?"

"Tell Tom what?" her bestie asked.

"About not being able to have kids."

Alex's face darkened, and she frowned. "Why would you ask me that?"

"Tom said he'd mentioned wanting a family," she said, averting her gaze.

Her best friend growled, her face red and angry. "As if I don't feel bad enough about it, now you're butting in?"

"Gene said Tom doesn't even want kids," Jessica said, trying to recover. She'd never seen Alex like this over something they both knew. She was the one with the short fuse, not her best friend.

"You told Gene?"

"Well, he asked, and I figured you told Tom last night and I didn't want Gene asking something like that," Jessica stammered, her stomach rolling.

"It's none of his business, Emily!" Alex threw the garbage bag down and stomped upstairs.

She'd gone too far. When Alex resorted to their first names, she was really upset. Jessia huffed. Why was her best friend so mad? It wasn't like it was a secret. Tom would've told Gene anyway, so why was Alex mad at *her*?

Jessica followed Alex upstairs.

She was throwing clothes into her suitcase, tears streaming down her face.

"So, what did he say when you told him?" she whispered, afraid to ask why her bestie was packing.

"That he wanted *me*, and that we'd just have to be a great aunt and uncle to your kid."

Jessica smiled. "That's good, right?"

Alex flopped down on the bed and put her head in her hands. "Yeah, but is he *really* going to be happy with that? I know he'd be happier with kids."

"It's not impossible for you, just difficult. You could go on hormone treatment or have in vitro," she suggested, sitting next to Alex and putting an arm around her.

"Yeah, but that costs money. Guess I'm going to have to go back to work."

"I thought you were going to raise horses to sell," Jessica said. Any job Alex got would take her away from the farm. She looked over at the suitcase, as if it would bite her.

"That takes a long time to make money. First, I have to get a good stud and that's going to be expensive, then it's eleven months gestation for a horse."

"Eleven months? Ugh! Nine is going to feel long enough," Jessica said.

A look of longing passed over Alex's face and she had an immediate pang of guilt. She wasn't intending to hurt her friend. She needed to change the subject. "So, where did you go last night?"

"The cave."

"What? Why would you go there?" She felt bile rise in her throat and had to swallow hard to keep from being ill.

"I go there a lot."

"Why on earth would you do that?" She barely held back a gasp.

"Something happened to me in that cave and I can't figure it out." Alex let out an exasperated breath. "When Tom was gone, it helped me feel connected to him. But now? I don't know. I guess I went looking for answers."

"Answers to what?" Jessica asked.

"I don't even know anymore." She sighed heavily. Alex was wearing a shirt and a pair of blue jeans. She had pulled her hair back into a ponytail last night. There were dark circles under her eyes, and she looked a little pale.

"Be honest with me. Are you all right?" Jessica asked.

"Yeah, it's just been a long night."

"How long has it been since you slept?" she asked.

Alex looked at her wrist but she wasn't wearing a watch. She touched the empty space, where paler skin revealed the outline of the missing piece. She let out a breath. "I don't know. Tom and I talked most of the night. I think I slept a little."

"You should rest," Jessica said.

"Now you sound like Tom," Alex said, voice irritated.

"Well, he's right. You'll never get your strength back if you don't rest."

"I will once we get this mess cleaned up."

"It's fine. I can handle it," Jessica said.

"Wouldn't work if I tried. You know I'd just lay down and feel guilty about not helping. No, I'll help you finish, then try to relax."

"Maybe by then the boys will be back and Tom can go rest with you." Jessica winked.

Alex laughed. "Yeah, I don't think he'd want to sleep."

She laughed. "That's not what I meant, but I heard you had fun yesterday."

Her bestie blushed profusely. "I thought you were asleep! Were we that loud?"

Jessica laughed again. "No, you weren't. I was asleep, but Gene was in the shower."

"Argh! I'll never hear the end of that then!"

Jessica smiled through the sudden guilt that rushed her. "I'm sure he won't tease you, Tom, maybe, but not you."

She shrugged. "Too late now to worry about it."

CHAPTER
SEVENTEEN

CHAPTER SEVENTEEN

Tom

Tom's heart sped up when he saw Alex was carrying out a garbage bag of what had to be broken things, as they pulled up to the house. He took in a deep breath, as if he was breathing her in.

"You all right, over there, Tommy?"

"What?"

His cousin smiled teasingly. "I swear, you're gonna come just watching her."

He punched him, hard but enough for Gene to know he didn't appreciate the comment, before he got out of the Mustang.

Alex set her bag down next to the other two by the garbage can.

"Looks like you girls have been busy," Tom said closing the distance to her.

She put a hand on her hip and used the back of the other gloved hand to wipe her forehead. "We're almost done. Jessica's just finishing the mopping."

"Alex, why didn't you get some rest?" he asked.

Alex met his gaze. The dark circles under her eyes and the droop of her shoulders told him she was exhausted. "I couldn't make Jessica do all the cleaning. I already took off last night and left her with the dinner mess."

Tom sighed and took her hand, then led her back to the house.

She didn't fight him as he led her upstairs.

Tom led her up to her room and dug through her drawers. He found her some underwear and a fresh pair of pajamas, then grabbed her hand and led her to the bathroom.

She still didn't resist, but she didn't really help him either.

He started the bath and added her bubbles to the water. He ran his hand under the water to check the temperature.

Alex's shoulders slumped forward, showing him how exhausted she was.

Tom rose from the edge of the tub and crossed the room to her. He tilted her chin up. "You should've rested," he chided.

"I can't sleep," Alex said.

He pulled the scrunchy from her hair, letting her dark hair fall around her shoulders. He slipped his fingers into her hair and massaged the back of her head.

Her eyes closed with the simple pleasure of it.

Tom slipped his other hand around her waist and pulled her into him. He kissed her softly.

She melted into him.

He kept his kiss tender and loving, trying to convey how much he cared about her in that one kiss.

Alex's eyes slowly opened when he pulled away.

Tom said nothing as he started methodically undressing her. He pulled off her shirt and unhooked the bra, tossing them into a pile.

She finally complied, unbuttoned her jeans, and slipped them off.

He smiled as he watched her strip.

She wasn't skinny, but he loved the curves of her body. When she was finally undressed, he helped her into the tub.

"Wait! You're not joining me?" she complained.

"Do you want me to?"

Their gazes met; her eyes were pleading.

Tom quickly undressed and slipped into the tub behind her. He pulled her back against him, massaging her shoulders to help her relax. "So why can't you sleep?" he asked, his fingers working at a knot in her shoulder.

"I'm afraid."

"Afraid of what?"

"I'm scared I won't wake up. That I'll be trapped in that cold, dark hole." Alex shivered and rolled onto her side, resting her face against his.

"I won't let that happen again." He stroked her hair. Tom held her tight for a few minutes, then spotted a washcloth hanging on the rack behind them. He grabbed it, dunking it in the warm water. He washed her body, moving her so he wouldn't miss a spot. He dampened her hair with the washcloth and shampooed her hair. "I'm afraid I have to get out so you can rinse that out."

Alex's eyelids drooped, so Tom almost had her relaxed enough to sleep.

He stepped out of the tub and dried off, wrapping the towel around himself while she rinsed her hair. He held a towel for her and dried her off, then helped her dress in the simple pajamas.

Tom led her back to her room, gathering all their clothes as they went. He closed the door to the bedroom and dropped their clothes in a pile by the bed.

Alex crawled into bed and had a look of surprise written on her face when he slipped his jeans back on. He buttoned up and slid into his shoes without lacing them.

"Are you leaving?"

He didn't miss the wavering in her voice. "I'll be right back. I need to grab something out of the car." He jogged to retrieve Gene's flask of whisky.

Tom grabbed a juice glass from the kitchen on his way back upstairs.

Alex was under the covers, lying on her left side, facing him when he came back in. "What's that?" she asked, propping herself up on her elbow.

"It's something to help you sleep," he said, pouring a little into the glass.

She took the glass and looked at the amber liquid. She swallowed the contents and started coughing. "What was that?" she coughed again.

"Whisky." He smiled.

Alex handed back the glass with a disgusted look.

He smiled again, and set the tumbler on the nightstand. He crawled into bed next to her and Alex lay down beside him. He took a deep breath and sighed. Tom couldn't imagine any place he'd rather be.

Tom held her as her breathing synced with his and she drifted off. He lay there, simply holding her, almost dreading what would happen next.

Gene

Gene found Jessica mopping the kitchen.

She looked up and smiled when she saw him watching her. "How did it go?"

"Oh, they won't be bothering you again."

"Good. I don't think I can afford to replace everything again."

"Did they break that much?" he asked.

She shrugged. "Mostly Aunt Marge's things, so it wasn't stuff I was super attached to, but I'm going to need a new sewing machine and some dishes. Don't suppose I could convince you to go shopping with me?"

"I might be open to that," he smiled devilishly.

"Then I'll just slip upstairs and change real quick," she said, leaning the mop next to the bucket.

"Can I watch?" Gene asked, smirking.

She swatted his stomach as she passed.

Gene chuckled and pulled out his car keys.

They drove into North Platte and found a mall.

Jessica went into *Bed, Bath and Beyond*. She studied different dish patterns. "I kinda like this one... Or maybe that one. What do you think?"

"Whichever ones you like would be fine," Gene said, not sure how to answer. This was so foreign to him.

"All right, would you your meals on these or these?" She held two plates out to him.

"Depends. What's on them?" He smirked.

"Gene Priest, I really want your opinion. Now please tell me what plates you like?"

He pointed to one and Jessica nodded, seeming satisfied. Like he gave a shit what plates she wanted, but at least it got the spotlight off him, and he did want her happy.

She picked up a box of the plates and moved over to the glasses.

Jessica found some glasses she liked, consulting him on those again.

He wanted beer mugs, but she just shook her head, making him laugh.

Jessica tried to balance the box plates and two boxes of glasses.

"Why don't you make yourself useful and go get a cart?" she teased.

Walking back to his woman, shopping cart in hand, Gene's phone buzzed in his back pocket. Reluctantly, he pulled it out, letting out a sigh before answering.

He knew reality would come crashing back into his life at any moment, but he wasn't ready to let go.

"Agent Cole," he said, answering the line one with one of his many aliases.

"We are calling today about your extended warrant--"

Gene immediately disconnected the line, letting out a deep sigh of relief. Although those types of calls happened rarely, he was beyond grateful this time for it.

He promptly made his way back to Jessica.

Gene pushed the cart around while she picked out a few other things. He smiled to himself. He hated to admit it, but he was beginning to enjoy himself.

When they finally checked out and headed out to the car, he spotted a baby store next door. "Did you want to go over there?" He pointed at the store.

Jessica's face lit up with one glance at the store, joy and surprise obvious by the widening of her eyes and the smile growing on her face. "Do you?" she whispered, her tone opposite her expression.

"We gotta get stuff, don't we?" he asked, his voice gruff to his own ears.

"Yeah but..."

"But what?"

"I didn't think you'd be into decorating the nursery."

"Well, it's part of it, isn't it? Besides, I have taken care of a baby before," Gene said.

Jessica tilted her head back and arched an eyebrow. Skepticism was written all over her pretty face.

He ignored her, putting the dishes in the back seat of the Mustang and locking it. Gene put a hand on her back between her shoulder blades as they headed in.

CHAPTER
EIGHTEEN

CHAPTER EIGHTEEN

Tom

The Mustang pulling into the yard woke Tom. He glanced at the clock. He and Alex had been asleep for about four hours.

Alex was snuggled against him, and he didn't want to wake her. She was finally sleeping peacefully.

Tom lay still, listening to the car doors slam, then the front door opened a few minutes later.

"Tommy, come give me a hand!" Gene yelled.

Alex jerked awake, jumping up to her elbow next to him. Confusion and fear laced her expression, and she frowned.

"It's okay, it's just Gene," he said, rubbing her back.

It seemed to take her a minute to process what he'd said, but then she collapsed back on top of him and groaned.

"How do you feel?" he asked.

"Tired," Alex mumbled, rubbing her face against him.

"Tommy! Come on!" Gene shouted again.

Tom groaned. "I'd better go see what he wants. Why don't you stay here and try to sleep some more? I'll be right back." He kissed the top of her head and slid out from under her. He jumped into his jeans and went downstairs right as Gene came in, carrying some bags.

"There you are. Grab your shoes. I need some help," his cousin said, dropping the bags in the living room.

"Gene, we gotta move that stuff out of the sewing room first and paint," Jessica said.

"I know, babe. I just want to get it all out of the car."

He arched an eyebrow. Did Tom detect a hint of apology in Gene's voice? Tom stared. He'd never seen Gene so compliant.

"Tom, grab your shoes!" his cousin barked.

Tom went back upstairs and grabbed his shoes from Alex's room.

She was lying on her side, facing the door.

"Go back to sleep. I'm just going to help Gene get some stuff out of the car and I'll be back."

"Tom?" she said hesitantly.

He turned back to her.

"I don't know how to tell Jessica I want to leave."

Tom smiled. "Don't worry, I'll think of something."

He headed back downstairs and blinked at the growing pile in the living room. He shook his head and went outside, so his cousin wouldn't order him around again.

"So, who bought all this stuff today?" he asked, as casually as he could. The trunk was packed full with a few more things in the back.

"Mr. Gary Gallahan is to be thanked. His $10,000 credit limit came in handy. The nursery furniture will arrive on Friday." Gene sounded smug.

That was something they had fought over more times than Tom could count. His cousin didn't see any issues with maxing out some poor schmuck's credit card, because the insurance would cover it. Besides that, hadn't they saved the world over and over, so there *would* be credit cards to use?

In Gene's mind, it balanced out. Tom disagreed and tried his best to persuade his cousin not to commit fraud repeatedly.

Gene had agreed to give it a shot, and for almost a month they'd lived on their own.

Tom had quickly learned that although they had "jobs," they never got paid. There was no way to continue hunting and saving lives with no income. He just hoped they weren't ruining lives in the process.

"You broke the cardinal rule, Gene. You left a trail."

Gene cocked his head to one side.

"Ordering furniture to be delivered. Now the credit company can trace it back to Jessica."

His cousin smirked. "Really? After all these years, do you think I'd make such a rookie mistake?"

"You've been acting differently ever since you found out you're going to be a father."

"Come on Tommy, you know me better than that. I got a cash advance on the card and paid with the cash, so there's no connection with the card."

Tom shook his head and took in a load.

Jessica

Jessica was in the living room sitting on the floor when Alex came downstairs. "Hey! Did you get some sleep?"

"Yeah," her bestie yawned.

"You can go back to bed if you want. I didn't mean to wake you."

"It's all right," Alex said, sitting on the floor beside her. "Look at all this stuff! What did you get?"

Jessica started pulling things out of bags to show Alex when Tom and Gene came in.

They set down more plastic bags. It took them a few more loads to get everything—the last was the five cans of paint.

Alex pulled gender-neutral outfits out of the bags, holding them up as she went.

Jessica smiled.

They giggled at some things Gene had picked out. One outfit was tiny blue jeans, a black bodysuit, and a green and black flannel.

"This is such a Gene outfit," Alex teased.

It warmed her heart, seeing a small light in her best friend's eyes.

"Are you hungry?" Jessica asked, putting her hand over her stomach. "Baby is starving."

"It's been a while since I ate, so yeah. Food sounds good."

She got out the leftover chicken and dumplings and reheated them.

Gene came in behind her and kissed Jessica's neck.

"It's not the best, but, understandably, no one's up for cooking, and there's nowhere to order pizza from."

"What about—"

Jessica quickly put two fingers over his soft lips to silence him. "Alex and I want nothing to do with the roadhouse right now, not after what had happened with Bill and Jack."

"Need help?" Alex asked, coming into the kitchen.

"Can you set the table?"

Her dearest friend nodded and got dishes to set the table. "So, what's the plan for painting?"

"If we work in teams and do two rooms at a time, it should only take two days at most to do the entire place," Tom said.

"That works!" Alex smiled.

"How about Tom and I clean up the dishes, so you two can head up and get ready for bed?" Gene offered after Jessica let out a big yawn at the table.

The girls got up and headed for the stairs. When they were halfway up the stairs, Jessica made a remark.

"I thought only bad girls get sent to bed early. I guess I'm a bad girl now."

"I heard that, Jessica!" Gene hollered.

She caught Alex's eye, and they laughed like schoolgirls.

Jessica closed the door to her bedroom and smiled. If Gene wanted a bad girl, she could certainly comply. Biting her lower lip as she pulled open her lingerie drawer, she pulled out a black lace teddy and her stockings.

She slipped into them, snapping the garters in place.

Jessica lit a few candles around the room, giving it a soft glow before sliding on her black heels.

*Gene

Gene left Tom to dry off the last of the dishes. He climbed the stairs and found Jessica's door closed. He knocked.

"Come in," she said, her voice hinting at seduction.

He opened the door and smiled. The light was out, and a few dim candles glowed around the room. His eyes moved to the bed where she stood next to it, gently holding the post with one hand, her hip cocked, drawing attention to her long legs.

"Damn!" he whispered.

"You said I've been a bad girl," Jessica smiled provocatively.

Gene grinned and pulled off his T-shirt. He moved closer.

She inhaled, her eyes clearly admiring his chest.

He stepped into her, intentionally taking her breath away with his kiss. He slid his hands over the lace of the cups of her bra, and one touch ignited his senses.

The entire room was intoxicating.

From the scent of the candles, enhanced by her feminine aroma, to the soft lights of the flickering flame, and the taste of her skin.

Gene was captivated by her. He touched every curve of her body.

Jessica moaned as his lips moved to her neck and shoulder. She tried to urge him onto the bed, but instead of sitting, he backed her up to the wall.

She undid his pants, pushing them down over his butt, just enough to expose his hard shaft.

Gene kissed her again. He cupped one breast and ran a hand down her leg, hiking her knee up. He worked his way around the thin strip of fabric between her legs, impaling her against the wall.

Jessica cried out in satisfaction, her head tilting back against the wall.

He thrust in and out of her, his body breaking out in a sweat as his soul rode hers. He could feel her getting closer to the brink, and her breath came in ragged gasps.

Gene lifted her other leg, pressing her to the wall for leverage as he drove harder, faster, bringing them both to a climax.

Jessica's body rippled around him as he exploded within her. She let one leg slip to the floor, and they stood together, panting.

The trees were thick and dense, hard to move through. Jessica pushed the foliage out of her way, her heart thundering in her ears. She needed to move faster!

She opened her mouth and took in a deep breath with the intention to scream her lover's name, but no sound emerged.

She tried again.

Nothing.

Seeing a break in the trees ahead of her, Jessica pushed harder. Her bare feet stung where the branches, barbs, and other debris of the forest floor cut her. But she couldn't stop.

Her baby needed her!!

Something moved to her left. Something sinister.

Ice-cold fear gripped her, causing her to stumble and fall, her hands taking the worst of the impact. Blood filled her palms.

Trying to get to a standing position, she was knocked back to the ground by an unseen force.

"The child is ours now."

The voice was raspy, wet sounding. And absolutely terrifying.

"Give me back my baby!" she was finally able to scream.

"Never. What we take, we keep."

NO!!

Jessica awoke to sunlight streaming in her window. Scrubbing at the sleep in her eyes, she was still shaking from fear. She took a handful of cleansing breaths before slipping carefully out from under Gene's heavy arm and went to clean up.

It took a while, but she finally rinsed the nightmare from her body and soul, ready to start a new day.

It was only a dream.

She dressed in grubby clothes for painting, and she headed downstairs.

Alex's door was still closed.

Tom probably had convinced her to stay.

It was a relief, for now.

She started breakfast and made coffee.

Gene came downstairs first. He was in jeans and still shirtless.

She admired his muscular chest as he reached for the cup of coffee.

"So, what do you want to do first?" he asked, leaning back against the counter and crossing his ankles.

What Jessica wanted to do was peel those jeans off of him and go at it on the kitchen table, but she fanned herself and went back to her cooking. "I think we should empty the room that will be the nursery first. Then we can do all the painting at once," she said, avoiding looking at him.

"All right, Tommy and I will get started on it after breakfast."

CHAPTER
NINETEEN

CHAPTER NINETEEN

Tom

Tom stretched as he woke. He smiled because Alex was curled up against him.

She woke up looking at him, still drowsy with sleep.

"Good Morning!"

"Morning," she replied.

"How did you sleep?" he asked.

"Surprisingly good."

"I told you I wouldn't let anything happen to you. I think I smell breakfast. Should we head downstairs?"

Alex groaned. "I was hoping we were going to run away together today."

"We will, but we should probably help with the painting first," he said.

She sighed and frowned.

"We'll go. I promise," Tom said, kissing her forehead.

She sighed again and rolled out of bed. Alex got dressed near the closet.

Tom dug through his bag on the other side of the room.

"Tom?" she said almost timidly.

"Yeah." When she didn't respond right away, he glanced at her.

"I don't know how to tell Jessica we're leaving. I'm afraid it will hurt her pretty badly. We always do everything together."

"But you still want to go, right?" he asked.

"Of course."

Tom smiled. "All right. I'll take care of it."

Alex sighed in relief.

After breakfast, Tom and Gene moved furniture out of what had been Tom's room when they'd first arrived. They put it in the storm shelter below the house, ensuring they had a place to sit if they were ever trapped in a storm.

Once that room was empty, they moved all of Jessica's sewing supplies into Tom's old room and set her up to continue her sewing business.

Alex had been painting the hallway, trying to cover up the threats that'd been spray-painted there. She finished upstairs and moved down to the lower level since the hallways would all be the same color.

Tom came to join her, picking up the nearby roller as she worked on the trim. "You're pretty good at this." He admired her skills with a brush.

She smiled. "One of my many talents."

He chuckled at her sarcastic tone.

"How's it going upstairs?" Alex asked.

"Good. We got everything moved out, so now they have to paint in there, then I figure we can get it set up in the morning and head out," Tom said.

"Did you tell them yet?" she asked.

"No, not yet."

"Tom!" Her irritation was loud and clear in her voice.

"Tell us what?" Gene asked from the stairwell. He was alone.

Alex blushed and looked back at her painting.

He rolled his eyes, because she'd fed him to the wolves. "I was going to take Alex for a little road trip. I thought we could use a little alone time," Tom said casually.

"Where would you go?" Gene asked, one eyebrow arched.

"I don't know, just a short drive. Maybe stay at the depot for a few days?"

"Oh!" His cousin said, his expression surprised. "Well, make sure she knows about the alarm system."

Tom didn't miss Alex's shock, as she was acting as if she wasn't paying attention to them. No doubt she couldn't believe Gene was actually giving his blessing for her to go to the depot.

"What alarm system?" Jessica asked as she came downstairs.

"To the depot," his cousin said. "Tommy is going to take Alex on a little road trip. Hey, you're not planning on taking the Mustang, are you?"

"No, we'll take my truck," Alex said, her cheeks bright red.

"Well, have fun," Jessica said, but her pretty face was guarded, and her tone had been unsure, or maybe even half-hearted.

"Thanks," his dark-haired beauty said, but her face was even redder.

Gene

After lunch they put on a second coat of paint, then Gene followed Alex out to the barn, so she could show him how to take care of the horses. He wanted to give his cousin the space they needed, but the thought of caring for Alex's horses had him worried.

Tom tagged along while Jessica went to rest. All the work they'd done had wiped her out.

"Check the trough every day to make sure they have enough

water," Alex said, as she showed him where the hose was. "I'm giving them a little alfalfa every day to fatten them up." She led them into the barn and broke off a large flake of alfalfa, handing one to Gene and one to Tom. She followed them out of the barn where the horses stood waiting.

Ellie whinnied at them, hoofing at the ground.

"Does she always do that?" Gene asked, hesitantly trying to offer her a snack.

Alex smiled. "Yeah, she's complaining we're taking too long."

Gene threw the flake to the mare when she wouldn't take it. He reached to pet her.

Ellie jerked her head away, laying her ears back briefly before returning to her food.

"Bitch," Gene mumbled. Not really meaning it, just frustrated that he had no game when it came to the large beast.

"Don't be such a jerk, Gene," Tom teased.

Gene watched Alex take Tom's hand, laughing at him as they headed back into the house. He should have been upset, but he couldn't help but to chuckle at himself over it. He'd fought just about every monster imaginable, but he was scared of a horse?

Not scared.

Unsure.

This was all new to him.

When they were done with horse care 101, Gene went upstairs to check on Jessica.

She was sleeping on her right side, curled up with her hand resting on her small belly.

A warm feeling spread through him, starting in his belly and permeating his entire being. He had never had such emotions rock him like this.

He wanted to reach over and move the tendril of hair that had fallen over her face, but kept his hands to himself, knowing his touch would wake her.

How did I get this lucky?

His eyes caught sight of the black teddy she had worn the

night before, crumpled on the chair in the corner of the room. Gene's cock jerked awake at the reminder of their passion.

Looking up at the ceiling, as if he could see to the Heavens, he whispered a silent thanks.

I don't know what I did to deserve this, but thank you.

Gene realized for the first time in his adult life, he wasn't itching for a new case. He was completely content living this normal life.

He knew it wouldn't last. Hunters were always hunters, and something inevitably would come crashing into their world.

But he would take every moment of this normalcy for as long as it lasted.

He slipped out of the room as quietly as he had entered and returned downstairs.

Tom looked up from the couch where he was flipping channels.

"She's out cold," he said.

His cousin smiled. "You worked her too hard."

Gene flopped down on the opposite end of the sofa. "I'll tell you what, man, I never knew I could worry about someone as much as I worry about her now."

"Aww, isn't that sweet," Tom teased.

He smacked his cousin's chest. "I'm serious, though. I never thought I'd be a father, but now... I'm going to have a little person to worry about."

"So what are you going to do? Retire? Hang up your hunting boots?"

Gene snorted. "Nobody retires from hunting."

"You could do it. It might be hard, but if you really wanted it—"

"I tried that, once, remember?" He rubbed his hands together. "It lasted about two months, then I was right back into it, with you in tow. I'm a hunter, Tom. I don't know how to be anything else."

. . .

Tom

Alex headed into the living room, carrying two beers by the neck in one hand and a bowl of tortilla chips in the other. She set down the bowl and handed the guys each a beer.

He couldn't tear his eyes off of her lithe form, even though she wasn't doing anything but walking into a room. "Thanks," Tom smiled up at her, warmth filling his chest at her kind gesture.

"You're welcome. Dinner's almost ready. Just a taco bar tonight, so you'll have to dish it yourselves, but I thought we could watch a movie."

"Sounds good to me," Gene said.

"Do you want to see if Jessica wants some?" Alex asked.

"I was just up there and she's sawing logs."

A look of concern creased Alex's brow. "Maybe we shouldn't leave the farm." She met Tom's eyes. "I don't want Jessica to wear herself out taking care of this place while I'm gone."

He glanced at his cousin.

"What am I? Chopped Liver?" Gene said, tapping his chest with a hand.

Alex worried her bottom lip.

"Don't worry, I'll take care of her," his cousin reassured her.

The worry in her dark eyes said she wasn't convinced, but she headed back to the kitchen, anyway.

"She doesn't trust me," Gene said, watching the door swing closed behind Alex.

"She doesn't trust anybody." Tom shrugged.

He cocked his head to the side. "She trusts you."

"Not always. She's used to making sure everything is done right, and she doesn't know how to let go. That's why I want to get her out of here for a bit. Being possessed by Judith really shook her up."

"Yeah, I can tell," his cousin said, following Alex's movement as she went into the dining room and set a couple of bowls on the table.

"Do you guys want to pick a movie? I'll just grab the rest of the dinner then we can eat."

"Sure," Tom said, heading over to the DVDs.

Gene followed, taking the other organized shelf.

"Let's watch this." Tom held up a DVD.

Gene leaned over to see what he'd picked.

"*Rustler's Rhapsody?* Never heard of it. How about this?" he said, holding up the *Bourne Identity*.

"Nah, Alex picked this movie up at the store when we were here in August. She said it's funny, and I'd rather have her laughing tonight."

The movie was still wrapped in the original cellophane, no one had even watched it yet.

His cousin conceded reluctantly.

Alex brought out the rest of the taco fixings and they each made themselves a plate. She set a bowl of guacamole on the coffee table next to the chips.

Gene eyed it suspiciously while Tom scooped some on his plate.

"It's just guacamole, dude."

"It's green," he said.

"Have you ever had fresh guacamole?" Alex asked.

"No, I stick to burgers and fries." Gene arched an eyebrow.

"Then you need to take a thank-you bite," she said, scooping a little onto a chip and handing it over.

"What's a *thank-you* bite?" his cousin asked.

"It's a bite you take to appreciate the person who took the time to make it for you. If you don't care for it, that's fine, but you need to at least try it."

Gene took the chip and obeyed.

Tom leaned forward, ready to smack his cousin verbally if the guy was rude.

Alex stared at Gene.

"Wow, that's really good!" he said, his eyes wide.

Tom smiled at Alex's expression of satisfaction.

She settled back on the sofa next to him and he started the movie.

Her brown eyes sparkled with joy when the opening credits scrolled across the screen. "You remembered!"

"Of course. You said it was funny, so I've been wanting to watch it," he said.

*Gene

Gene was enjoying the movie until Alex tucked her toes under his thigh. At first, he flinched, and was going to call her on it, but one glance told him she probably wasn't aware.

Her body was stretched out, and she was snuggled into his cousin, sleeping.

He smiled and grabbed the blanket off the back of the sofa and covered his cousin's girl.

She was visibly exhausted, with dark circles under her eyes and calluses on her hands.

Tom had told him Alex was a strong woman, but until now, he hadn't given her due credit.

Jessica had said she felt guilty leaving so much work to Alex, but she'd been so tired lately, so she hadn't helped keep up with her share. No wonder Alex didn't trust him to take care of things while she was gone.

Well, I'll just have to prove her wrong.

It was still early when the movie ended, and Gene wasn't actually tired.

Tom carried Alex upstairs to bed.

Gene hung out on the sofa, channel surfing for a few. Then he cleaned up the mess left from dinner.

When he heard someone coming down the stairs, he snapped his gaze over to the stairs, his body ready to pounce if need be.

Jessica stepped into the living room, looking adorably warm and sleepy in crumbled PJs. "Why didn't you wake me?"

Gene smiled. "You needed to rest."

"I hate being left out," she pouted.

"You didn't miss much. We just ate and watched a movie." He handed her a plate. "I'll go warm up this meat for you."

Jessica filled a plate and sat on the sofa with Gene, eating in silence while he channel surfed.

They lay on the sofa watching a movie on TV.

Contentment settled over him, making his heart race. It felt perfectly normal it felt, having a movie night, on a couch, in an old house, with his baby mama curled up next to him.

"Please, let me keep this. Haven't I earned a moment of peace?" Gene whispered the words, unsure who might hear them, but hoping something on their side did.

CHAPTER
TWENTY

CHAPTER TWENTY

Alex

Alex awoke bright and early the next morning. She was energized and ready to go, hoping to finish the nursery so she and Tom could head out.

She pictured what it would be like to have a normal life with Tom. She could see him coming home from a long day of work, tired and worn out, and she'd rub his shoulders to help him relax while dinner finished cooking.

Alex sighed as she climbed out of bed to get dressed. It was a fantasy. For one thing, she didn't really know how to cook, and if she started massaging his shoulders, it'd probably lead to other things, and she'd forget all about dinner. Not to mention the reality of Tom's job.

He was a hunter. She couldn't ask him to walk away from that. There were other people out there who needed his help, and she couldn't ask him to give that up for her.

Alex stripped out of her pajamas and looked for clean clothes. Her face overheated when she turned around.

Tom was lying with his hands folded behind his head, a smug look on his face.

"I thought you were asleep," she said.

He smiled but said nothing.

"Why didn't you say something?" Alex asked.

"I was admiring the view."

She shook her head. She was no supermodel. She didn't even like to look in the mirror alone naked.

Tom climbed out of bed. He wore pajama pants but no shirt.

Her body responded to his. She bit her lip and couldn't tear her eyes away from him stretching. Sadly, he headed out of her room, likely to the bathroom.

As soon as he was out of sight, she let out the breath she'd been holding. She still couldn't believe he wanted to be with her, but she'd enjoy it for as long as it lasted.

She could smell bacon and pancakes cooking. Her stomach growled with the prospect of eating. Throwing on some old jeans and a tank top, Alex hurried downstairs to join Jessica in the kitchen.

"It's not quite ready," her bestie said. "If you wanna go see if the guys could use some help, I only need ten more minutes."

Alex made her way back upstairs, to find the guys working in the room that would become the nursery.

"Grab a roller," Gene called out. "This should be the final coat."

Alex had barely started on the wall when there was a loud knock on the front door. They had no trouble hearing it upstairs.

"Boys! The crib is here!" Jessica yelled.

Alex set her paint roller on the pan and stuck her head out the door.

"Dude, come on, you gotta check this out!" Gene said, smacking Tom's arm as he took off down the stairs.

Tom shook his head and met her eyes. He shrugged.

"I guess he's excited," Alex said, smiling.

He leaned over and kissed her cheek before following his cousin.

Since the walls weren't quite dry, they stacked the furniture in the living room until they could assemble it. They all ate a hearty breakfast, then the guys started to assemble the crib in the living room.

"Are you sure you want to do that down here?" Alex asked.

"Well, we can't do it in the room cause the walls are still wet," Gene said.

"But it's going to be harder to carry up the stairs that way."

"It's alright, we're big strong guys," Tom teased.

Alex just smiled. "My two cents… If I was doing this, I'd carry the box upstairs and assemble it in the middle of the room, then put it in place when the walls dried. But you've got to figure it out for yourselves." She headed upstairs to clean up and pack.

No matter how careful she was painting, she always managed to get paint in the oddest places. She had a shower and slipped into a pair of bike shorts and a tank top while she packed her suitcase.

Alex smiled as she heard the frustrated arguing between Tom and Gene while they tried to assemble the crib.

"I think they might kill each other." Jessica leaned on her door frame, looking childlike in her denim overalls and her hair in pigtail braids.

"Nah, they'll figure it out." Alex chuckled. "They haven't killed each other yet. I doubt building a crib will be the straw that breaks the camel."

Jessica came into the room and sat in the chair at Alex's vanity, putting her hand protectively over her growing tummy. "Are you really going to leave me?" her bestie asked, her voice clearly not holding back her emotion.

Alex let out a deep breath. She'd prepared herself for this conversation. Maybe. "I just need a break. After what Judith did…"

"She wasn't trying to hurt us," Jessica defended her great-great-grandmother.

"I know, but—" She let out a frustrated breath. "You don't know what it was like to have to watch helplessly as your body is used and you can't control what's happening or even let anyone know it's not really you. And then to be trapped all alone and not know..." Alex's breath started coming in shorter gasps. She took a deep breath and shook her head to clear the memory and tears as she grabbed some more clothes from the closet. "I just need some space. Please understand."

"I know, I'm sorry. It's just, I'll miss you. So much. I've never been alone with Gene, either."

"Is that what you're worried about?" Alex asked, meeting her best friend's gaze.

Jessica's expression betrayed her concern. Her aquamarine eyes were filled with tears, and her forehead was wrinkled with what must be trying to hold back the waterworks.

"Oh, Jessica, he loves you. You're going to be fine."

"It's just that I've been trying so hard to keep him happy, you know?"

"Why do you feel like you have to try? He's here, isn't he? And no matter what you two *don't* have in common, you'll always have one important thing you share," Alex said, indicating her belly. "He didn't freak about the baby, either."

Jessica smiled and rubbed her hand over her belly. "Yeah, we do. And you're not wrong. It went better than expected, for sure."

———

An hour later, Alex heard the loud swearing carrying up the stairs. They stepped out of Alex's room to see the guys bumping the edges of the crib against the freshly painted walls and the rail, leaving scuff marks.

She smirked. She'd tried to warn them.

Both guys had broken a sweat by the time they got it wrestled into the room.

Jessica moved around the banister and into the room to decide where to put it.

Tom came out of the room. "Whoa, I'm getting out of here!" He grinned. He stopped in his tracks when he spotted her.

There was no doubt that she had an "I told you so" look on her face. Alex had no regrets about that.

She'd changed into a simple black dress that flared out just above her knees. Her hair was in ringlets framing her face, and her makeup done, complete with bright red lipstick.

"Well, you were right about the crib," he said, walking around to her, a smile slowly spread across his face.

"About what?" she said, playing innocent, and arching an eyebrow.

"You know exactly what," Tom said, pulling her into his arms. He leaned down and kissed her. "You look nice."

"Thanks," Alex whispered. "You don't think it's too much?"

"Too much for what?" he asked, his brows drawn tight.

"For going to the depot."

Tom smiled. "This is just for me?"

"Well..." She stared into his hazel eyes. Her face flush with heat, not to mention her lower regions.

"How long do you need to pack?"

"I'm packed," she said.

"Really? Well then, I guess I'll grab my stuff, and we can head out."

Alex's heart soared.

CHAPTER
TWENTY-ONE

CHAPTER TWENTY-ONE

*Jessica

A tear slid down Jessica's cheek as she watched Alex and Tom drive away.

Gene stepped up behind her and wrapped his arms around her. "They'll only be a couple of hours from here. Don't worry. Tom will keep her safe, and I'm here with you."

"I know, but she's like a sister to me, and I'm so used to her being here."

"Now you'll have me all to yourself," he said, kissing her shoulder.

"Really?" she teased. "And what will you do with me, now that you have my undivided attention?"

"Well..." He kissed her shoulder close to her neck. "I was thinking..." Gene kissed the soft skin where her shoulder and neck met. "...that I would start..." He kissed the side of her neck when she tilted her head away to give him better access, "...by peeling these clothes off you." He sucked on her earlobe, eliciting a moan from her.

He turned her in his arms and picked her up, carrying her across the threshold into the house and up the stairs to her room.

Gene set her down right in front of the bed, encouraging her to sit on the edge.

The moment Jessica did, he got down on one knee and reached for her left foot. He slipped the black ballet-style shoe off, kissing her ankle before he released her.

He took her right foot and did the same. This time, his kiss on her ankle was just the beginning.

Gene lifted the edge of the leg of her overalls and continued kissing up, sending delicious shivers over Jessica's skin.

When he couldn't go any further, the denim bunched up as far as it would go; he slipped the opposing fabric back down and stood up, offering her his hand.

Jessica stood, holding her breath when he unhooked the left side of her overalls, tossing the strap over the shoulder.

He promptly did the same on the other side, causing the garment to fall to the floor in a pile of indigo.

She stood there in a white, sleeveless, button-up shirt, white bra, and red panties, feeling more exposed than she'd ever been. Jessica had been naked with him before, but it was different this time. She couldn't explain why.

Gene reached for her shirt to continue undressing her but fumbled with the tiny buttons. "Son of the bitch," he mumbled.

"I've got this," she whispered, swiftly slipping the buttons through the holes. She didn't remove the shirt, though, allowing him to go back to his fun.

He'd slipped his shirt off while she'd worked on her small task. He leaned forward, slipping his hands behind the open shirt to bring her closer, allowing their bodies to meet, even if for only a moment.

Gene took his time shedding off her top before he kissed her bare right shoulder, followed by the left. His hands slid up the skin of her back until he reached for her bra and unhooked it.

Jessica sighed with the instant relief one gets when removing an over-the-shoulder-boulder-holder. Being pregnant had made her breasts larger and heavier. The hormones flushing through her at the moment were making them tingle in a way she had only experienced when she was alone and thinking of Gene.

She let the bra slip to the floor to join her overalls.

Seeing the look of lust in his vibrant green eyes just about sent her over the edge. Those orbs trailed down her body, and it was obvious he was taking in the subtle changes to her body.

Jessica wanted to squirm, a little self-conscious of the fullness of her curves, but quickly reminded herself she was growing another human and it was perfectly normal for her to have a bit more of everything.

Besides, her love seemed to like what he was seeing.

That made her heat all over, revving up a notch.

Gene ran his fingertips down all the places his eyes had just roamed.

Her panties got moist from the anticipation. Sex while pregnant was an entirely new thing, and the most erotic feelings swept over her.

Her skin tingled even after this touch moved to a new place. She'd likely climax before he made his way below her waist.

He didn't need to touch her most sensitive spot to send her over the edge.

Jessica gasped when his thumbs skimmed the overly sensitive nipples, causing them to pucker into tight little nubs. "Gene," she moaned.

He answered her by taking her right breast into his hot mouth.

Her nether regions quivered, threatening to explode in pleasure while he gently sucked and flicked the pink nub. He released her, but took the other nipple into his mouth.

Her core tightened, and the buildup of an orgasm began.

Gene flicked, teasing with touch and tongue.

Jessica's muscles tensed as her body exploded with the most intense orgasm she had ever experienced. She cried out and ecstasy washed over her.

Her legs buckled and Gene had to catch her before she went down.

"Holy shit, babe. Are you okay?" he asked, actual fear in his voice.

Panting, she replied. "Oh…yeah…I'm…great…"

He guided her back to the bed, insisting she be on more stable ground.

Jessica moved up the mattress, resting her head on her pillow in the center of the bed for a breather.

Gene removed his jeans, freeing the part of his body that hers was crying out for.

Her red panties were still on, and she was in great need of having them removed. She slipped her thumbs under the waistband, intent on removing them, but he quickly joined her on the bed, straddling her, preventing her from going any further.

He replaced her hands with his own. "I started this. I want to finish it." Inch by slow inch, Gene slid the damp fabric down her legs, slipping each foot out. He tossed the panties over his shoulder, not bothering to see where they landed.

More heat rushed her all over at the hungry look he gave her. He wanted her as much as she wanted him, and she loved that.

Jessica loved him.

Gene slipped his hips gently between her legs, his erection caressing her core.

"Gene," she whispered again. "I can't take much more."

"Oh, baby. I'm just getting started."

In a good way, but it was going to be a long night.

Gene

•   •   •

Gene kept his weight off of Jessica, even though his arms were burning from holding him up. However, it wasn't just her he was protecting anymore. He had to think of their child, too.

Our child.

He still couldn't believe those words.

Even though there was no doubt about the child that grew within his woman's womb. He had a moment of guilt, or maybe fear.

Would making love hurt the baby?

If so, it was already too late, since he'd taken Jessica against the wall the night before.

He was being ridiculous. She was fine and loved every moment of that, and she was loving this too.

He would be gentle this time, and really make love to her.

Gene looked at his lady love, naked as the day she was born, all curvy and stunningly beautiful. Every change he noticed was just another piece of proof she was carrying the future—his future.

Her breasts were at least one or two cup sizes bigger. Her nipples looked different. Where they'd once been a perfect color match to her full lips, they now were a slightly darker shade of pink.

He leaned down and kissed her, their tongues dancing, her hands exploring the muscles of his back. He could feel the tension in his shoulder blades from holding his own weight up, and she seemed to find the exact spot, trailing her fingers.

Gene broke the kiss, moving down her body, trailing a hot path with his mouth and tongue. One on her chin, another on her neck.

A kiss in the valley of her breasts caused a sigh from her lips.

He kissed her ribcage on the left side, then her hip bone, stopping for a moment to move up to the small mound that rested above her pelvic bone.

Kissing from one side to the other, he stopped right in the

middle and whispered to the growing child. "I love you, little man. And I will always protect you."

"Gene," Jessica whimpered. "It could be a girl," she chided, but her voice was thick with desire.

"I know." He grinned.

She reached for him, delving her fingers deep into his hair, running her nails lightly over his scalp, which brought gooseflesh to the surface and made his cock jerk in anticipation.

Gene continued his exploration of the changes in her body. He kissed the top of her pelvic bone, then the top of her right thigh, then her knee, her calf, then the top of her foot.

He switched sides, starting with the foot, making his way back up her legs, stopping at the very top of her thigh when Jessica cried out.

"Gene! I really can't take much more!"

He ignored her pleading, fully intending to have her begging for another release in the next few moments. Gene did just that. The moment his mouth touched her core, her back arched, and a scream came from deep in her throat.

Gene licked and flicked and sucked as her body orgasmed, her sheath pulsating with her pleasure. He took that moment to insert one finger, then another, feeling her muscles tighten and grip his digits. He kept them still, waiting for the aftershocks to subside.

As soon as her muscles were spent, he began his torture again, pressing upward on her G-spot, watching her face for telltale signs she was about to come again.

"Gene!"

He wanted her to climax again, waiting so patiently for the right moment to join her in bliss.

When her back arched, or her legs went rigid, she was so very close.

When she started showing that sign, he moved with speed and plunged deep within her, letting her body squeeze him with the contractions of another orgasm.

Gene didn't move, resting while she panted through the next

round of aftershocks. "Are you ready?" he asked when Jessica was finally still.

"I can't take much more," she panted.

He chuckled and dipped down, taking her mouth again. Gene began a very slow and gentle rocking, moving with complete purpose.

This was about pleasing her, making sure she was fully sated.

He needed to wipe away the tears of the day, with her best friend leaving. Even if he could make her forget for one night, that would be a start.

Jessica wrapped her long legs around his waist, giving him deeper access to her, locking her ankles.

She was ready for all of him.

He moved deeper and faster, feeling her taking him all the way to his balls.

Their kisses, combined with her tight body, brought on his own climax sooner than he'd expected. His sac jerked and tightened, seconds before his own orgasm exploded.

He rode it out, letting her body milk him for everything he had.

Gene had wanted her to climax again. The moment he stopped moving her muscles tightened around him.

She had joined him, after all.

CHAPTER
TWENTY-TWO

CHAPTER TWENTY-TWO

*Alex

Alex let Tom drive her truck. He seemed to enjoy operating the four-door Dodge Ram as they headed down the dirt road away from the farm.

She didn't miss that he kept sneaking looks at her as they drove.

It'd been a tearful goodbye for her and Jessica. She blamed her bestie's hormones because it wasn't until Jessica started crying that Alex had teared up as well.

As they drove past the roadhouse, her heart rate picked up, and she fidgeted in her seat.

Tom took her hand. "They can't hurt you anymore."

She smiled, half-heartedly. "I know." Alex turned on the radio. She took a deep breath and sighed as the country music filled the surrounding silence.

They stopped for a leisurely lunch, followed by some shopping, before they headed to the depot.

Even though the drive itself was just over two hours, the multiple stops made it several hours later when they made it to the sleepy town of Esbon, Kansas.

Tom had told her they preferred to arrive after dark to avoid people seeing them, finding out they lived there. He pulled up to the backside of a one-story brick building, driving up a ramp and parking under the awning.

Alex took in the dilapidated exterior of the train station with all the windows boarded up. "Umm… Tom, what are we doing here?"

"This is it. The depot."

She looked him up and down, glanced out the window that the old place, and then met his eyes again. It looked terrible.

"Come on." He chuckled and got out of the truck. "I'll show you." Tom grabbed her suitcase and his duffel bag from the back of the truck.

Alex grabbed her computer bag.

He waited for her at the front of the vehicle and took her hand.

The door creaked from lack of being used.

She followed him through the old station, behind the counter to a door with a padlock on it.

He pulled out a set of keys and opened the door. It opened on a small landing at the top of a flight of stairs. Tom flipped on a light.

The door opened onto the landing of a flight of stairs. To the right, the stairs opened up into a room the width of the building.

"Welcome to the Esbon Train Depot," he said, leading the way down the stairs. He set their bags down at the bottom of the stairs.

Alex looked around. To her left was a small seating area with two wingback chairs and a small table. To the right was a long table with six chairs. There was one ramshackle bookcase on the wall behind the table, full of books that overflowed to the floor and table.

"This is the library," Tom said.

She arched an eyebrow.

Sheepishness and amusement darted across his tempting mouth. "Okay, one bookcase and stacks of books aren't exactly a library," he admitted, then led her through the next room. "Here's the kitchen."

She glanced over the outdated kitchen before he continued the tour of the depot.

"And this is my room," he said, pushing open the first door on the left.

The room was so sparse; it was no wonder he preferred to stay in her room back at the farmhouse.

The painted cinder block walls were a tan color that was depression alive. There was a queen-sized bed and single night-stand, a small chest of drawers, a wardrobe, and a desk with a chair.

"Not very cozy," she said.

"We aren't really here all that much and mostly we just need a place to sleep that isn't the car." Tom shrugged.

The room was like a time portal into the 50s. All the furniture was antique but well-maintained.

Alex stepped into the room and ran a hand across the beautiful wood of the desk. There were a few books lying there, one was open. She looked down at the drawing of a hideous monster.

She closed her eyes at the reality of Tom's life. If she wanted to be a part of it, she'd just have to toughen up. After all, a ghost had possessed her, so what could be worse?

Tom stepped up behind her and leaned down, kissing her bare shoulder.

She rolled her head to the side to give him better access. She savored the feeling.

They were finally alone.

Home?

At least for a while.

Somehow, it made her feel…good and bad.

Alex didn't want to feel.

Not right now, anyway.

His hands slid down the black material of her dress that hugged her curves, finding the button holding the halter of her dress up.

He slowly slid the zipper down her back. "I love that you're not wearing a bra," he whispered in her ear. Tom turned her and kissed her passionately while he worked the tight dress from her body.

Alex pulled his shirt over his head, relishing the feel of his bare skin on hers.

He kicked off his boots and shucked his pants, pulling her back against him. Tom slid his hands down her body, removing her silky panties in the process.

He picked her up; she wrapped her legs around him.

She thought he'd carry her to the bed, but he turned and pressed her back against the closed door.

He impaled her there.

Alex cried out at the feeling of him inside her.

Tom held her to the wall with his arms as he slid in and out of her.

She'd never experienced anything like this; her body exploded in orgasm after just a few strokes.

He held her still while her body pulsed around him. He buried his head in her shoulder.

"Tom, are you all right?" she asked, still gasping for breath.

He slid out and carried her over to the bed. He lay down on top of her. "I love you, Alex," he said, meeting her eyes.

"I love you, too, Tom." Alex ran her fingers back through his hair. "Can we just stay here forever?"

"Only if we get a new mattress." Tom smiled. He leaned down and kissed her again.

She moaned against his mouth as he slid into her again.

Alex matched his rhythm as his orgasm built. As her body rippled around him again,

Tom released himself into her, moaning in ecstasy. He collapsed on top of her, his energy clearly spent.

She trailed her nails up and down his back. She loved the feel of his weight on her.

Tom relaxed, falling asleep on her chest.

Alex enjoyed the quiet and his rhythmic breathing. She didn't have to worry about anything scary attacking them here.

Tom had explained all the wardings they'd put around the depot.

"I think I could really like it here," she whispered to the man sleeping beside her.

Tom

Tom woke up about an hour later. He was hungry. He and Gene had been gone for a few weeks, so there was nothing edible in the kitchen.

He tried to ignore the growl in his belly. He slipped out of bed, careful not to wake Alex, but he watched her for a minute and smiled.

He'd never seen her so relaxed. She really had been so tense living in the farmhouse.

Tom got dressed and left a quick note in case she woke while he was gone. He took her keys and headed out, calling in a takeout order to his favorite restaurant in town. To be fair, it was the only restaurant in the tiny town, but the food was great.

His dark-haired beauty was still asleep when he got back. Alex lay on her stomach with her arms wrapped around the pillow, the sheet pulled up just enough to cover her butt, leaving her back exposed.

He crumpled up the note and tossed it in the garbage can, then went to her side of the bed. Tom sat next to her and ran his fingers through her hair.

Alex slowly opened her eyes and smiled at him.

"Hi," he said.

"Hi." She yawned, and it was as adorable as she was.

"Are you hungry?"

She rolled over, pulling the sheet up over her breasts. "Yeah, I could eat."

"Good, I got dinner. Would you like to come eat with me?"

"I should probably get dressed."

"Clothes are optional. After all, it's not like anyone will walk in on us." Tom smiled.

Alex shook her head, but got dressed quickly.

He hated to see her cover up, but loved the pajamas she pulled from her suitcase. It was a good sign that she was going for comfort. Tom led her to the library and began pulling white containers out of a paper bag.

"Wow, how much food did you get?" Alex had wide eyes.

"Well, I wasn't sure what you liked, so I got a little of everything. Burgers, salad, chicken wraps. Besides, with our extracurricular activities, you might be hungry later." He waggled his eyebrows.

Alex giggled, and it made his smile wider.

He was so damn happy,

As they sat at the table and ate, she quizzed him about hunting and his life here in the depot.

Tom answered all of her questions honestly. He wanted to protect her, but keeping things from her could get her killed, and he didn't want that.

"So, you don't mind if I check out some of these books?" she asked.

"Actually, it would be nice to have someone to do research with. Gene has a limited attention span when it comes to books. He's all about the action and wants to get right to the fight, but we have to know what we are dealing with first, and how to kill it."

Alex continued to eat, but her expression was intense, with furrowed brows, letting him know she was processing this new information. "I don't think I'd be very helpful in a fight, but if you could teach me how to defend myself, then I might feel like I could be of *some* use to you," she said finally.

"You are more than use to me Alex, I love you."

She smiled and his heart skipped at the love on her pretty face.

Tom squeezed her hand. "One step at a time. You need to know what you're fighting before you worry about how to fight it. That's where Gene always fumbles. He wants to get right to the action, without the education first."

"I think I can handle that," she replied.

CHAPTER
TWENTY-THREE

CHAPTER TWENTY-THREE

*Alex

They spent three relaxing days just enjoying each other's company. Alex read some of the books of mythology to familiarize herself with Tom's world. They were both in the library reading one morning when Tom's cellphone rang.

Alex stared as he listened on the phone.

"Yeah, I can come up. No, it's not a problem. I think I should check it out... Okay, thanks." He hung up and met her eyes. "Well, so much for taking some time off," he said, sighing.

"Who was that?" she asked.

"Stacey. She's a sheriff in South Dakota. She has some suspicious disappearances going on and she wants Gene and I to check it out."

"All right. Are you going to pick up Gene on your way up there?"

"No, I'll just head up there. It's probably not anything supernatural anyway, but it never hurts to check it out."

"How long will you be gone?" she asked.

Alex's tummy churned. She didn't want to be in the depot alone, and she didn't want Tom to go into potential danger alone, either. Besides, if he took her truck, she'd be stranded here.

Could she go with him? Could she ask? Did she *want* to go?

"Do you want me to take you back to the farm before I head up there?" he asked.

"No!" She shook her head.

Tom cocked his head to one side. "Do you want to come with me?"

Alex swallowed, and her heart skipped. "I don't want to get in your way while you hunt." She averted her gaze.

"Well, it's a long drive and you could always stay at the motel while I go actually check out the disappearances."

She took a breath and smiled. "If I won't be too much of a bother..."

He leaned over, kissing her. "Babe, you could never be a bother. Besides, I'd love to have you come with me. And I'm sure Stacey would love to meet you."

They each packed a bag, and Tom loaded some weapons into the toolbox of her truck. He'd said he brought a variety since he didn't know what they'd be up against.

He'd told Alex he'd typically be researching the job on the way there while Gene drove, but since he'd be driving this time, he'd just have to get his info when he got to Sioux Falls.

Alex offered to research for him, and Tom had just smiled.

He drove into town and found a cheap motel. He checked them in and carried their bags to their room.

"So, what happens now?" Alex asked.

"Well, I need to go see the sheriff and find out what's going on. Gene and I find we get better results if we go as FBI agents."

"But she already knows who you are, right?"

"Yeah, in this case."

"Then why pretend? I mean, she's the one who called you here."

"It's not for her. We don't want to spread panic by telling everyone the things that go bump in the night are real, so we come in as FBI and that clears the way with the rest of the sheriff's office and takes the responsibility out of her hands. If something were to go wrong, she could just say the FBI took over, and she was following orders."

"I see." Alex nodded. It did make sense.

"If you have something business-like to wear, you're more than welcome to come," Tom said.

She chuckled. "You think you can pass me off as FBI?"

He pulled a wallet out of his bag and smiled. He handed her a folded leather wallet.

Alex gasped. "You made me a fake badge.?"

"Well, I didn't think it would hurt to be prepared. Besides, I may need you to interview witnesses, and this will help."

She took the ID from him and studied it.

"Alexandria Johnson?"

Tom flashed a grin.

"Where did you come up with that?"

"Well, I know your first name is Jade, but this way I can still call you Alex."

"And Johnson is so it's an easy alias?"

"Actually, Brian Johnson is the lead singer of AC\DC."

She laughed. "Yup, definitely on the Highway to Hell, now."

Alex went into the bathroom to freshen up while Tom changed into his suit.

He was just tying his tie when she stepped back into the small room.

She wore a black pencil skirt and a red blouse. She'd styled her hair in a French twist, giving her a very professional look.

"Wow! You look amazing," Tom said.

Alex touched her cheeks, which were already burning. She

went over to her suitcase and pulled out her black jacket that turned her skirt and blouse to a business suit. "Ready?"

Tom smiled and took her hand leading out to the truck.

They walked into the sheriff's office, and all eyes turned on them.

Alex's heart hammered, echoing in her ears. She took a deep breath and followed Tom up to the counter.

"I'm looking for Sheriff Martin," Tom said, sounding all business.

"Who's asking?" The deputy asked, putting his hands on his belt, as if challenging Tom.

He flipped open his badge. " Special Agent Young. This is my partner, Special Agent Johnson."

"What the hell's going on here?" A uniformed female stepped into view. She was taller than Alex, but not by much. Her brunette hair was kept short, and her hazel eyes were sharp.

Alex felt herself take a small step back, feeling the aura of authority oozing from this woman.

"Rick, are you just going to stand there holding your pants up, or get these nice agents some coffee?"

The deputy grumbled under his breath and headed to the back.

"Thank you for coming, agents. If you'll just follow me, we can have a seat in my office."

*Tom

Tom gestured for Alex to walk in front of him.

Stacey led them into a back office and closed the door. As soon as they were alone, she gave him a big hug.

"How are you?" he asked.

"Can't complain. Although being a mother to two teenage

daughters is a lot to handle. And who's this?" The sheriff asked, smiling.

"Stacey, I'd like you to meet Alex."

Despite her open expression, she frowned. "Where is Gene?"

Tom smiled. "Gene's, uh…spending some time with someone special."

"Well, good for him. Alex, are you a hunter too?" Stacey asked.

"More of a hunter-in-training," she said.

"So, what seems to be going on?" Tom asked.

The sheriff sighed and went to her desk. "We've had four people go missing in the last couple of months."

"What makes you think it's our type of thing?" he asked.

"The first body just turned up," she said, handing him a photograph.

The man had a sickly white complexion and was thin, as if someone had sucked all the fat from his body. His eyes had dark circles, and someone had left him in a heap of brush and branches, partially hidden.

He met the sheriff's eyes.

"He was exsanguinated. Some…thing drained all his blood."

The color drained a little from Alex's face when she looked at the picture.

The man's skin stretched tightly across his face, as if dehydration and heat had affected him.

"What do the victims have in common?" Tom asked.

"Nothing that I can tell," Stacey replied. "This guy was a business executive and an athletic health nut. He went missing first. Then a homeless guy who had a camp outside of town. Then a stripper from Maurice's and now a kid from Chrissy's school."

Stacey handed Tom the files she'd started for each of the victims.

He handed a couple of them to Alex the way he would to Gene, as he sat in the chair across from the sheriff. Tom scanned all the information on the first two victims. The man worked as a corporate executive for a big company downtown, lived in a gated community, and was a member of a country club.

He wore dark blue jogging pants and a white T-shirt like he'd dressed for a run, and they'd discovered him in the same clothes. An empty white wireless earbuds case had been in his pocket.

The second file was for the homeless man. He was a Vietnam veteran who hadn't been able to hold down a job since he returned from war.

Tom looked over the files, looking for common denominators.

Alex had the third file, and when she handed it to him, he quickly scanned it.

The victim was a stripper who'd lived in a single bedroom apartment within walking distance of the club. The police had arrested her for drug possession and prostitution in the past.

The fourth file was of a girl from Chrissy's school, who is an introvert. Gothic and socially awkward, most of the kids had shunned her at school. She kept to herself and didn't speak much.

"What else can you tell us?" Tom asked.

"Not much, unfortunately. Parents reported the kid missing when she didn't come home after school. Our corporate guy was reported missing by his wife. She said he went for his evening run and never came home. Got an anonymous tip about the stripper who turned out to be another stripper friend of hers. Said she hadn't shown up for work in a few days."

"What about Herbert?" Alex asked.

Tom glanced at her, arching an eyebrow. She'd sounded so serious, as if she was working the case, and not just hanging with him to see what he did.

"Herb was a good guy. He was a little paranoid after the war, so he didn't like to be around too many people at once. I took groceries out to his campground about once a week and checked on him. A couple of weeks ago, I stopped by, but he wasn't there. I figured he just went into town for something, which he did on his good days, so I left the groceries. When I came back a couple of days later, the groceries were still where I left them."

"Any chance he just left town?" Tom asked.

"No, he grew up here, and it's where he felt safe," Stacey said.

"What about the girl?" he asked. "Any chance she's a runaway?"

"I'm hoping so, but I didn't want to take any chances."

"Where did you find the body?" Alex asked, without looking up from the files.

"Outside of town, some workers found it in a ditch near the old foundry," the sheriff said.

"Okay, we'll check it out and let you know what we find." He climbed to his feet.

Alex glanced up and handed the files back to Stacey with obvious reluctance.

"Keep 'em," Stacey said. "Maybe you'll see something I didn't."

Alex smiled and tucked the files against her torse.

Tom held the door for her as they headed out.

"Tom?" Stacey called.

He lifted his chin.

"I have a roast in the crock pot. Why don't you guys join us for dinner? I'm sure Chrissy and Sophie would like to see you again," the sheriff smiled.

"That sounds great. Thanks." Tom smiled and headed out.

CHAPTER
TWENTY-FOUR

CHAPTER TWENTY-FOUR

Gene

Gene watched with fascination as the tech ran the wand over Jessica's growing belly.

The doctor explained what they were looking at.

"That is a beautiful spine. I think the baby is going to be on the long side."

"Long side," Gene asked, automatically thinking of the male anatomy. "That's my boy."

The doctor chuckled. "Um, not that kind of long. I mean the length of the baby at birth. We say 'long' not 'tall' as our description."

"Oh," Gene muttered, feeling his face flush red in embarrassment.

The sound of the rapidly beating heart grabbed his attention, sending him over the emotional edge. He couldn't stop the tear running down his cheek, unfortunately exposing his tender side.

The little bean that would one day grow into a full-size human was *his*.

Gene still couldn't believe it. He watched the screen, looking at the baby moving around, stretching out, and making its presence known.

He forced his eyes away from the monitor to look at his beautiful woman.

Jessica watched in awe at the thing he'd been glued to just moments before. Her cheeks flushed pink, and it was obvious she was excited to look upon their child.

"Things are looking good," the doctor said. "There's no sign that the fetus suffered any damage from your incident two weeks ago. Baby is right where we'd expect it to be at this time. The due date shouldn't change. We are still looking at March Ninteeth."

"That seems so far away," Gene said.

"It goes by faster than you think," the doctor said. "Have you started prepping yet?"

"I'm just over halfway, and we've already put the crib together," Jessica said.

"That's a start. Make sure you get signed up for the Lamaze classes. We recommend you start them at twenty-four weeks."

Gene looked at Jessica, completely out of his element. He frowned. "Um, what's Lamaze?"

The doctor laughed. "Don't feel stupid on this one. Most dads have no clue what that is. It's a technique of breathing that helps mothers during the birthing process. Dad is most often the coach for mom, reminding her how to breathe through the pain with each contraction. It's unbelievably helpful."

He just nodded. He didn't get it, but wasn't willing to share that information. Gene glanced back at the image of his child on the screen. "When will you know if it's a boy or a girl?"

"I don't want to know," Jessica said.

She liked to plan things out; it was one of the few things she could have control over. So, this baffled him.

"What?" he asked. "Really? Why not?"

She took his hand. "For one thing, I know you can be overly protective. And I worry that if it is a girl, you will be impossible to deal with."

"It doesn't matter what the baby's sex is. I will be overly protective of you and our bean. Always."

The doctor stepped closer, handing Gene the small roll of printed photos of his growing child. "Through the ultrasound, it's too early. Only by a week or two, though. Now, we could do blood work and tell you. But mom says no. And what mom wants…" She shrugged and smiled, gesturing to Jessica.

"Fine. But have I mentioned I hate surprises," he grumbled.

"Poor Gene," his love teased, wiping the last of the jelly off her little bump. "Sucks to be you right now."

"I'll see you back here in another four weeks. Once you're over thirty weeks, I want to have you come in weekly. We usually push off that often until the last four weeks, but with your history, I'd rather keep a closer watch on you." With that, the doctor left, the tech on her heels.

Jessica got off the table and got dressed. "I don't know about you, but baby and I are starving."

Gene leaned in and kissed her softly on her bare shoulder while she hooked her bra back together. "Oh, I'm hungry, all right," he whispered, with a nip to follow the kiss.

"Burgers, Gene. I'm hungry for burgers."

Jessica

With a belly full of food, she was ready for a nap. Growing a baby was exhausting work. However, she had things to do.

The doctor talking about getting things prepared for the baby made her realize how much she needed to do to get the old farmhouse ready.

She'd read in a book that once the kid was born, the time to get things done was pretty much non-existent. Jessica wanted the place toddler-proof well before the baby was even born, and not take chances, even though they would have months before crawling.

In the house's library, she stared at all the things on the lowest levels of the wall-to-wall bookshelves. Most of the trinkets that'd once been in the room had been destroyed by the vandals weeks ago.

Fortunately, the vandals hadn't tampered with the books and journals. With the empty spaces in between books, there was now space to move everything up. She couldn't just stick them anywhere.

Jessica liked an organized bookshelf.

Pulling books from the bottom shelves first, she opened each one to glance at its contents before placing it in a pile. She discovered printed novels, vintage encyclopedias, farmers' almanacs, and personal journals among the books. Each different style book went into its corresponding pile.

"What do you think you are doing?"

The book in Jessica's hand went flying into the air to land with a heavy *thunk* on the hardwood floor.

The deep timber of his voice had her jumping out of her skin.

"Damn it, Gene! You scared the shit out of me!" She stood, dusting her hands on her maternity jeans.

"I thought you were heading upstairs to take a nap. That's the only reason I stayed outside to work on the car. You should be resting." He wiped his hands on a rag that might've been baby blue at one point in its existence. Gene had a small smear of grime on his left cheek.

She should've thought he was filthy, but his dirty black T-shirt that was clinging to him in all the right ways had her hormones raging.

No, not right now, girl. I've got to get this room put back together.

"I said I could use a nap, not that I was actually *going* to nap. I have too much to do today," she said, spreading her arms out to indicate the mess she'd made.

"Let me get washed up, then I'll come and help." Gene whirled without waiting for her to reply and stomped up the stairs.

Jessica could smell Gene's freshly showered scent moments before he entered the room. Every little thing about him seemed to set her aflame. She felt like a teenager with her raging hormones.

All she wanted to do was strip him bare, work him up to a sweat, and lick him like a lollipop. It took all her strength not to do just that.

He wore dark blue jeans and another black T-shirt.

She really needed to get him to try out other colors. His wardrobe pallet was so dreary. Black… black… black.

Oh, and a splash of dark green or burgundy. Gene would occasionally toss a dark-colored button-up over his black T-shirt. Christmas was only a few weeks away. She'd have the perfect opportunity to upgrade his wardrobe.

"Looks like you've put a dent in this chaos." He gestured to her organized piles.

"Well, I got the encyclopedias put in order on the third shelf. Can you believe they are from the 1940s? There is so much misinformation in here. I had to stop looking through them because I was getting angry. Did you know they thought fresh air would cure TB? They had no clue it was an airborne disease."

"Um, I didn't know that. What is TB?"

"Seriously? Tuberculosis."

"Oh," Gene said.

"I'm thinking we can do the novels next," Jessica gestured to the next pile. "Those need to go on the very top. I am trying to keep it all above the third shelf. That way, the baby can't pull anything on top of themselves once they start walking."

"Love, do you really need to worry about that right now?" Gene stepped up to her, helping her get to her feet.

"Yes. If I don't do it now, I may never get another chance."

He dipped down and kissed the top of her nose, sending shockwaves over her skin.

She was so sensitive that the slightest touch could make her nether regions quake. Jessica put her hands on his chest and gently pushed him away. "None of that. I've got to get this done."

"None of what?" His eyes were wide, but genuinely innocent. He really had no idea what she was talking about.

"Hanky-panky," she said.

"Jess, babe. That wasn't hanky panky." Without warning, he swept her into his arms, bent her backward, and kissed her like it was his last kiss ever.

When he let her go, she was panting, her entire body vibrating with need. "Gene," she could barely whisper his name.

"I know. We've got to get this done." Gene turned to the pile of novels, grabbed two handfuls, and lined them on the top shelf.

Jessica watched him for a moment, trying to get her overheated, hormonal body, to calm the fuck down.

Gene's lack of organization skills was the cold shower she needed. He was setting the books up willy-nilly.

"No!" she barked. "They need to be organized alphabetically. Either by title or by author. I haven't decided yet."

"Damn, honey. You didn't need to yell at me." He set the book he held gently back onto the pile on the floor. "How about you sit here, on the floor, and hand me the books, telling me where you want each one?"

That sounded like a great idea. She could work, and stay off her feet. Jessica skimmed through the pile on the floor. They were almost all different authors. So, organizing them by title would be better. "Right of the dark blue one," she said. "The other dark blue, on the left side. This goes right after *Treasure Island*."

They'd just about finished putting away the novels when Gene's stomach let out a loud protest. It'd been late afternoon when they started, and it was close to dinnertime. The obtrusive sound that came from the gorgeous man standing in front of her said it was time to stop.

For now.

"Can we call it a night?" Gene pleaded after they'd finished dinner and cleaned up the mess. He was downing a beer while she was trying to finish one more bottle of water.

"Soon. I want to look through the journals and figure out how I want them organized."

He wore a deer-in-the-headlights look, his head cocked to one side. "Um, wouldn't by date be the only real option?"

"I guess so." Jessica picked one up. The tan leather was a beautiful caramel color. She opened it up and thumbed to a random page. She recognized Great Aunt Marge's handwriting.

"Jenifer came to visit. It's been almost twelve years since she was last here with her husband and child. Emily Jessica is growing so fast. She looks just like mama did at that age. Grams says she is a special child. I know she is. I was there when they brought her to join us. Jenifer didn't know. She still doesn't know. I don't think she'd understand."

"At least now we know your great aunt wasn't crazy. Your great-great-grams *was* talking to her all along. Might change how you look at these journals now." Gene had stood behind her, his hands on her shoulders while she read.

Now it felt like he was holding her up.

"But she still sounds crazy. Mom said I had only ever been here once, when I was twelve, right before my thirteenth birthday. But this reads like I was *also* here as a baby." Jessica put the book on the empty shelf. She picked up another one. The leather was so old it was a dark coffee color.

• • •

"Judith gave birth to a baby girl last week. Sickly little thing. I don't think she will make it to the spring. Winter babies rarely do. Judith is adamant she will survive. We've named her Barbara, after my mother."

Gene read the text over Jessica's shoulder. "This must've been written by George. Well, we know Barbara survived." He flipped to the front of the book and pointed out the family tree they had seen in the journal over four months ago. "See," he said. "She married Otto, and they had a son, Henry, who died at fifteen." He closed the book and put it on the left side of the previous journal.

"Something seems off, don't you think?" Jessica asked.

"No. Times were different then. But it looks like you've got some great family stories to read over. Not tonight, though. You need to stop pushing yourself so hard. We've got four months to get ready for this baby. Let's take it day by day, please."

She looked into his green eyes and it hit her, as she studied his piercing gaze.

This was the closest thing to normal he'd done his whole life.

Jessica needed to let him find that normalcy and own it. Her weird past could wait for another day.

CHAPTER
TWENTY-FIVE

CHAPTER TWENTY-FIVE

*Alex

When they got back to the motel, Tom went to the restroom and changed out of his suit. When he came out, Alex was sitting propped up on the bed with the files spread out beside her and her laptop in her lap.

"Whatcha working on?" He flopped down next to her.

"I'm trying to see if there's a connection of the victims in location, since they don't seem to have anything else in common. Different ages, genders, social lives—it seems like they were victims of opportunity rather than by a specific trait."

Tom scanned her screen.

She'd brought up her maps and started dropping pins where the victims lived, worked and went to school. Alex had also marked the location where the victim was found.

He smiled.

She hoped she was impressing him. She was trying to think like a hunter.

"That's true, but it could all be that they are the same blood type, were hexed or they all had a specific encounter in their past."

"What kind of specific encounter?" she asked, frowning.

"Well, like they all witnessed a murder, or they all have the ability to see ghosts—could be a lot of things."

She sighed, overwhelmed. "How do you narrow it down?"

"I start with the victims, like you are. The guy they found was drained of blood," Tom said, grabbing his laptop and going into teaching mode.

"So maybe a vampire?"

"That would be the first logical choice, but we've killed vampires and they leave a messy aftermath, often tearing the throat out. This guy looks like he baked in the sun."

"So something that drains all the fluid from the victim and essentially sucking the life out of it," she said. This was both sickening and fascinating at the same time.

Tom scanned through several websites. "It could be a Djinn," he said, changing screens again.

"What's a Djinn?"

"Some think it's like a genie that grants your wishes but we've run into them before and they put you into a dream where your deepest wish comes true and it feeds off you while you sleep."

"How do you know that?" she asked, tilting her head up and narrowing her eyes.

Tom met her gaze. "Gene got caught by one. I barely got him back."

Alex swallowed audibly. She didn't know what she'd do if something happened to Jessica.

"We should probably get going soon. Did you want to change before dinner?"

"Yeah, that's a good idea." She jumped up.

Tom smiled as he held the door of the truck open for her.

She'd changed into a pink summer dress. Alex stepped out of

the truck, taking his offered hand. It was nerve-racking going to the sheriff's house for dinner, but this was a friend of Tom's.

A teenage girl with long blonde hair answered the door. "Hey." Her voice was somber.

"Hey," Tom said, more cheerfully.

"Where's Gene?" she asked.

"Nebraska."

She eyed Alex suspiciously.

"Chrissy, this is Alex," Tom said, gesturing to her.

"It's nice to meet you," Alex said.

Chrissy just nodded and walked back into the house, leaving the door open for them.

Tom placed a hand on Alex's back and guided her into the house. He closed the door behind them, then took her hand, leading her toward the kitchen.

She smiled and squeezed. It was like he could sense her discomfort, and she needed that when she was in a stranger's house.

Chrissy didn't seem to want her there.

Stacey was working in the kitchen. She smiled when she saw them. "Good, you made it! Dinner will be ready shortly. Tom, there's beer in the fridge. I don't know what Alex likes to drink."

He opened the fridge and grabbed a beer and a bottle of Moscato. He went right to the cupboard that held the wine glasses and poured her a glass.

How many times he had been here?

What exactly was his relationship with Stacey? She was older than him but a beautiful, slender woman with short dark hair, and Alex frowned.

Jealousy swam in her gut, chasing away some of her hunger.

"Here, Tom, you slice the meat while I finish getting this on the table, then we can eat," Stacey said, carrying two bowls of mashed potatoes and carrots to the table in the dining room.

Tom handed Alex the glass of wine and sliced the roast.

"So, how did you two meet?" Stacey asked when they were all seated around the table.

A dark-haired girl who'd introduced herself as Sophie had joined them, and the five of them had gathered around the dining table to eat.

"We met in a bar," Tom said.

Stacey frowned. "No offense, Alex, but what were you doing in the kinda bar these guys hang out in?"

Alex smiled. "Actually, it was the only place we could find to eat that wasn't an hour's drive away."

"I see," Stacey said, with a knowing look.

"Tom actually volunteered to come help us with a ghost that was haunting our place," Alex said.

"Now, that sounds more like them," Stacey said.

"Why didn't Gene come this time?" Sophie asked.

Tom and Alex exchanged a look.

"Gene's with my friend, Jessica. He's helping her fix up some rooms in the house," she said. Tom didn't mention the baby, so she didn't want to either. She'd follow his lead.

"I thought you were more of a handyman," Chrissy said.

"Well, you know Gene taught me most of that stuff I know," Tom said.

"So, any ideas on what we're looking for here?" Stacey asked, changing the subject.

"I think it's a Djinn," Tom said.

"Never heard of that," Stacey said.

"They put their victims into a trance where they fulfill their deepest wishes, while the creature feeds off them. Depending on how many victims they have, they can keep them alive longer to feed off them. If he really has three people right now, then there's a good chance they are all still alive," Tom said.

"But not for long," Chrissy said.

Tom's brows drew tight.

What kind of mother would teach their kids about this stuff?

"You're not really a hunter, are you?" Chrissy asked.

Alex shook her head.

"Well, an angel killed my dad, and a monster killed my mom. Sophie's family were all vampires that made her lure victims to their house."

Alex swallowed and licked her lips. What horrors these girls had endured. She threw Tom a glare. He should've told her. "I'm sorry. I just thought you were Stacey's daughters."

"We are now," Sophie said. "She took us in when we had nowhere to go."

Alex glanced at the sheriff, seeing her with a deeper appreciation.

"I'm no saint. I just had room, so it made sense," Stacey said. She shrugged, like she was trying to downplay what she did.

Alex smiled. She was starting to like this woman. She liked the fact that Stacey didn't want to be the hero.

"Do you have any idea where he's keeping them?" Stacey asked, changing the subject.

"I think it's in the foundry," Alex said.

"The foundry?" Stacey asked.

"Yeah. Alex found that all the missing people seem to have that place in common," Tom said.

"When are we going after it?" Chrissy asked.

"*We* aren't going anywhere," Stacey said in a mom voice. "Tom, Alex, and I will handle this."

"When are you going to accept that I want to hunt?" Chrissy shouted, planting her fists on the table.

"When you're eighteen and move into your own place," Stacey said, her voice betraying that they'd had this conversation before.

Alex ate silently as they waited for the family argument to dissipate.

Tom cleared his throat. "Chrissy, I really wish I could convince you not to hunt. But... I also understand your desire, since your family was taken from you when you were young. I simply wish to spare you the horrors of it. Hunters never retire, they never get to live in peace, there's no happy ending. You kill things until one of them gets you."

Alex felt bile rise in her throat. She knew the life of hunters was scary, but to hear him say this, at a family dinner, really hit home.

Jessica and her baby!

The fear of something happening to her bestie and the unborn child she carried had her covering her mouth to prevent herself from being ill. She took three very deep, cleansing breaths, doing her best to calm her racing heart.

"So the foundry?" Stacey said, getting back to the subject.

"Yeah. I'm going to go check it out tomorrow," Tom said.

Alex was hurt that he implied she wouldn't be with him, but she said nothing. Maybe he didn't want to volunteer her for something she wasn't ready for.

"I can come with you if you want," Stacey said, sipping wine.

"Thanks, I'm just going to scout it out first. But I'll call if I need backup."

"Yeah, right! You and Gene think you're invincible, but one of these days, you boys are going to need some help." the sheriff frowned.

"I promise if I find something, I'll call you." Tom nodded, his gaze earnest.

"I'll keep an eye on him," Alex said.

That seemed to settle the matter for Stacey. When they got ready to leave, Stacey shook Alex's hand and told her it was nice to meet her, then she gave Tom a big hug, planting a kiss on his cheek before she let go.

The moment they were in the truck, Alex went silent. Her thoughts were racing.

Maybe I would have been better off at the farm. I shouldn't be here.

She stared out the window, but instead of seeing the world outside, she was focused on the reflection of Tom.

I love him. I know I shouldn't get attached. Baby or not, Gene and Tom won't always be around.

Alex tried not to think of all the ways he could die, and tried to redirect her thoughts.

Thinking about how the evening went, she quickly went down another less-than-stellar rabbit hole.

CHAPTER TWENTY-SIX

Gene

Gene sat in the driver's seat of his Mustang, staring at the front door of the old Ferguson farmhouse. His beautiful woman was asleep inside. He still couldn't believe this was his life—for the moment at least.

This was a place he'd never dreamed he'd ever be. A situation that could be considered "normal life" kind of stuff.

He needed a place to think that was his old normal. His vintage Ford had been 'home' more than and brick and mortar location had ever been.

Gene had started out lying in bed beside Jessica, his mind racing a million miles an hour.

Jessica's soft snoring had been a sweet comfort most nights, but tonight, with the moonlight shining in through the light curtains, he wasn't finding comfort. He'd discovered a new fear brewing below the surface.

"What have I done?" he whispered to the dashboard. "I am in

no position to be a father. I've never even had a dog. I can barely keep myself and Tom alive. And now I have to keep Jessica *and* a baby safe? How?" Gene slammed his hands on the steering wheel, letting a fraction of his anxiety out.

Part of him wanted to call Tom.

His cousin had been his sounding board, having two years of college life before things had taken a drastic change; Tom had always seemed like the smarter one. However, he couldn't bother him. Tom was probably fretting over the same things, except not a baby.

They needed to figure things out on their own.

Gene ran through all the hunters he had met over the years. Not a single one of them ever had a family. It was one-night stands when they came. Love 'em and leave 'em. It was the safest thing. Never meant to hurt the other party, but simply to fill a carnal need and move on.

Tom had learned to hard way. There was a girl he'd met a few years ago, and he hadn't wanted her to only be a one-night stand. He'd fought with Gene about it, taking off for a week with her. However, when a group of vamps they'd been hunting found out about her, his cousin had had to watch as they held him down and tore that girl apart.

He'd probably never get over that. Not completely.

At daybreak, they'd let Tom go and told him that this was the same pain they endured every time one of their nest was killed. He'd suffer their pain until they met again. Rage filled, Tom had returned to Gene and they'd eradicated the nest, killing them all.

Gene was still in awe that after all that, they were open to— well, whatever *this* was.

He couldn't put a simple label on what he and Jessica had. He'd never been someone's 'boyfriend,' and that word didn't seem right for what they were. He was more than her baby-daddy.

Gene was her lover.

Her protector.

He loved her.

He'd die for her.

He looked up at the ceiling of the car, praying it never would come to that.

"How can I keep them safe?" He buried his face in his hands as he muttered those words.

Ultimately, he knew the answer.

He couldn't.

Just like anyone, there were things out of one's control. People died in car accidents every day. There were illnesses and cancers that no one saw coming. There would always be something.

Gene just prayed it was 'normal stuff'. Not something supernatural he could've killed.

There were now wardings painted on the walls that should keep anything from entering the house. No one would even know they were there. He'd painted them on with blue-light responsive paint, visible only when a blue light was shining on it.

He'd covered all his bases, from demons, to angels, to ghosts, and ghouls. Nothing should be able to penetrate the house. It was one small thing he could do to keep Jessica and their child safe.

He simply had to convince her to never leave the house.

Yeah, right.

Gene sighed and climbed out of the car. He needed to get some sleep.

Jessica had plans for them in the morning, and it'd take all his brain power to get through it. She wanted to go through the enormous pile of family journals and document the important stuff into a file on her computer.

Tom would have *loved* doing something like that. To Gene, it was pure torture. However, he would do it for her.

The stairs creaked when he made his way up.

Jessica was still quietly snoring, curled up on her side, her back to him.

Gene stripped down to his boxers and crawled into bed, fitting his body to hers like a perfect piece.

He wanted to stay like that forever.

This felt safe.

However, it couldn't last.

Jessica

"We need to stack them in chronological order before we begin digitally organizing them. Otherwise, we may miss something vital." Jessica had pulled all the leather-bound books off the neatly organized shelf and left them in a disheveled pile.

They *had* all been in order, but she'd removed them the night before, rearranging the shelves a third time.

Her new baby book said it was called 'nesting.' It was normal for pregnant women to do. She was simply doing it sooner than most women. However, she excused herself, seeing that she'd only lived in the house for four months.

So, pregnant or not, she still had a lot of settling in to do.

Jessica had re-arranged the cupboards in the kitchen four times already, and she still wasn't happy with the flow of things but had walked away to work on something else.

The journals had fascinated her since the night she and Alex had arrived, but Jessica hadn't had time to really delve into them. It'd been nagging in the back of her mind.

This was something she *really* needed to do.

She felt like something was calling to her, that she was going to get answers to questions she didn't know she had.

"Damn baby hormones," she mumbled.

"What's that?" Gene asked, thumbing through a journal.

"Nothing. I was just thinking aloud."

He raised an eyebrow in obvious expectation.

"No, Gene, that was *not* what I was thinking. Not this time, at least. I really need to get through these, plus it will help me stop thinking about Alex."

Gene put the journal down he had in his hands and wrapped his muscular arms around her. "Tom won't let anything happen to her, I promise. Besides, don't you think we have all earned some alone time? Now, you can scream out my name while I give you the most intense orgasm you have ever had."

Not only Jessica's cheeks heated, but her neither regions as well. She wanted so badly to take him up on his offer, but... "Thank you for that glorious visual I don't have time to think about, Gene. I'd love to get naked and let you have your way with me, but we need to get through these. There are close to fifty journals here. I don't think I need to document everything, but there's enough vital information in the pages here to take me weeks to get typed up."

Her lover let out a deep sigh, releasing her, and picking up the journal he had previously deposited on the coffee table. Gene opened it up and read from the first page.

"July 24th, 1895. Mama gave me this beautiful journal for my birthday. She said she still could not believe I made it to eighteen without a single marriage proposal. Little does she know, George Ferguson has all but beaten up any man who dares to look my way. He told me when we met, I was going to be his wife someday. I think he's going to ask Daddy for my hand this weekend at the county fair. George has a hog he's sure is a shoo-in for the blue ribbon this year..."

"Do you think that's the first one?" Jessica asked when he stopped reading.

He closed the journal and set it back on the coffee table. "I think so. But let's get them in some sort of order before we jump knee-deep into this. Are you really sure you want to do this now? It's gonna take weeks to get through all this."

"Gene Priest! I need to—" she stopped mid-sentence.

"You need what?" he prompted.

"I.. um… I just realized I don't know your full name. How can I chastise you without knowing your full name?"

He laughed heartily, sending waves of heat over Jessica's already overheated body.

"Yeah, I guess you'd need to know the whole thing in order to thoroughly yell at me." He took a deep breath and slowly let it out. "It's Gene Benjamin Priest."

"Benjamin? I like that. Maybe we can keep that in mind if the baby's a boy."

"Let's not worry about that right now. Like you said, we need to focus on these." Gene spread his arms out, showing the mess of journals on the floor.

"You're right. So… where were we?"

CHAPTER
TWENTY-SEVEN

CHAPTER TWENTY-SEVEN

*Tom

Tom's thoughts were completely consumed by the Djinn on the drive back to the motel. He didn't even notice that Alex wasn't talking.

He parked right in front of their room and held the door open for her.

She walked in and looked around the small room.

Tom wrapped his arms around her from behind. He sighed and leaned down and kissed the top of her head. "Penny for your thoughts?"

"How do you know Stacey?" she asked quietly.

Tom released her and took a seat on the bed a couple of feet from her. "You already know Stacey"s the sheriff here. We met her on a hunt a few years ago."

Alex nodded and headed for the bathroom.

Tom grabbed her hand as she walked by. "What's wrong?"

"It's nothing." She flashed a fake smile.

He frowned. "Doesn't seem like nothing."

She swallowed audibly and averted her gaze. "I know I'm not the first girl you've been with. I just didn't mean to meet any of them."

"What do you mean 'girls I've been with?' You're not talking about Chrissy, are you?" Tom asked, rearing back. "She's not even eighteen! I'm not a pedophile." He was half-crushed, and half-insulted.

"Not Chrissy. Stacey."

He arched an eyebrow. "Stacey? Why would you think that I'd been with Stacey?"

"You're comfortable in her home, and you know where the wine glasses are kept. You told her you'd call her if you needed help on the hunt, and then she kissed you when you left. Not to mention she's beautiful, smart, and isn't afraid of monsters," Alex blurted, her eyes misty.

Tom spread his knees and pulled her to stand between them. "Stacey has been a friend of Gene and me for a long time. I always thought she and our hunter friend, David, would get together, but it never seemed to work out for them. Alex, I love *you*," he said squeezing her with his legs. "Not to mention, she's too old for me."

"Then why don't you want me to help?" she asked. "I know I sound like I'm whining, but I can't help it. I feel like my world is falling apart, and I'm clinging to you like a life preserver."

"What're you talking about? You are already helping. It was you who saw the pattern and figured out where the Djinn was."

"But you said you'd call her if you needed help."

"Well, it would be silly to call you if you're with me."

"But you said that *you* were going to check it out tomorrow, not *we*."

Tom sighed, again. He was frustrated but didn't want her to feel bad for feeling insecure. "I don't want to encourage Chrissy to hunt. I know she wants to, but she still has a chance to have a real life, not live how Gene and I do. If I included you, then it would just mean that I am teaching you how to hunt. As it is now, they just think you're my girlfriend and along for the road trip and research help."

"You never told them we were together." Alex wore a deep frown that was really more of a glare.

He smirked. "Is that what this is all about? You're jealous?"

She nodded.

Tom pulled her down into his lap so he could look into her eyes. "You have nothing to worry about. I want to be with you. I've never taken anyone on a hunt and certainly not taken anyone to the depot. We haven't even told Stacey about it."

Alex finally smiled. "I'm sorry. I guess I just don't know how to fit into your world yet."

"You will. Or we'll make a new one of our own."

She leaned in and kissed him.

Alex

Alex woke the next morning with her head pounding. She grabbed some Excedrin before taking a hot shower.

"You all right?" Tom asked when she came out of the bathroom.

"Yeah, just a headache."

"Do you want to stay here while I go check things out?"

"No, I'll be fine."

"Are you sure? It's okay if you need to rest," he said, his brow furrowed in concern.

She smiled. "I took something for the pain. I'm waiting for it to kick in."

He studied her with his head cocked suspiciously.

"Come on, let's go check things out," she said, leading the way out the door.

They drove out to Herbert's campground, parking across the street in a dirt parking lot next to the park.

They checked around for any signs of foul play, but everything looked as if he'd just walked away from his meager belongings.

Alex pulled out her laptop, setting it on the hood of the truck. She brought up her map. "It looks like the running trail where our jogger disappeared is over that way." She pointed east of the camp.

They headed toward the trail and looked around.

Tom stepped away for a moment, stopping to pick something small off the ground. He returned to her; his hand held open.

A white wireless headphone sat there.

"It looks like we got the right place."

"Are you sure it's his?" she asked.

"No, but it is the type he wore, according to the file."

They both looked toward the foundry. It was dark and ominous, even in the early morning sun.

"Maybe we should call Gene," Alex said.

He met her gaze. "You don't have to go. I'll go check it out."

"But what if something happens to you?" she asked.

"I've been hunting most of my life. Nothing's going to happen."

This is a bad idea.

"I'm just going to go look around and see if I can tell where he's keeping the victims." Tom rubbed his hands from her elbows to her shoulders. "Trust me, I can handle this. It's what I have been trained to do."

He's so confident, but something feels wrong. Maybe it's just the headache coming on.

"I just have a bad feeling," she said. Alex's words didn't convey what she was feeling adequately.

He kissed her forehead. "I'll be back in a few. I'm just going to look around. Wait here. Don't worry. I'll be right back."

Alex watched him walk all the way to the foundry until he

disappeared around the corner of the building. She sat down on a nearby log and started working on her laptop.

*Tom

Tom searched for an easy way into the building. He could break through any number of the boarded-up doors or windows, but he didn't want to alert the djinn to his presence.

He worked his way around the back and found a door that wasn't boarded up. Tom quietly slipped through the doorway and worked his way into the foundry. Scrap metal was scattered throughout the rooms, along with large vats used for melting down the metals to reform them. He worked his way from room to room looking for where the djinn kept his victims.

A noise coming from another room off the main factory floor caught Tom's attention. He ducked behind some shelves and watched.

The Djinn came out of the room and looked around. He seemed to listen for something.

Tom waited quietly until the creature left, going outside. He dashed to the doorway. There was a large open room with a vaulted ceiling and bay doors on the outside wall.

This must have been the receiving dock. One, two, three, four. He got another one Stacey doesn't know about yet.

Four bodies were chained to the cement piles holding up the ceiling. They were all dirty and unconscious.

He approached cautiously, not wanting one of the victims to call out and alert the Djinn. He bent over the first victim to check for signs of life.

Something sharp slid into his ankle, and white-hot pain shot into his calf.

He spun quickly enough to spot an enormous snake slithering away.

Tom collapsed to the floor as the venom raced through him.

The snake dissolved into smoke that rose and coalesced into a man with blue markings all over his gray skin.

"Tom! Tom, wake up!"

He struggled to wake up. He was in a bed in a room he'd never been in before. Tom sat up, when she stepped into the doorway.

"Are you going to sleep all day?" Alex asked.

"What happened? Where am I?" he asked.

His dark-haired beauty came to him, sitting on the edge of the bed, tucking her dress under her.

"Are you all right, honey? Did you boys drink too much after your hunt?"

"What hunt? How did I get here?"

Alex just smiled. "Gene dropped you off. I'm not sure what time exactly, but I heard the Mustang and felt you crawl into bed."

"Gene! I need to call him!" Tom said, reaching for his phone on the nightstand, but she grabbed it first.

"You'll see him soon. You need to get in the shower right now, or we're going to be late."

She stood and went to the closet. "Hurry, Tom! I'll get your clothes lain out."

Tom frowned, but he got in the shower, anyway. The sooner he could talk to Gene, the sooner he'd figure out what was going on.

CHAPTER
TWENTY-EIGHT

CHAPTER TWENTY-EIGHT

*Gene

"All right. You want me to read these to you while you type it into your laptop?" Gene asked, while thumbing through another leather-bound journal.

"Unless you have a better idea. Then I can pick and choose what information's important." Jessica sat on the couch, her laptop balanced precariously on her knees.

"Not to sound like a jackass, but aren't there places that can scan the pages, turning it into digital files?" He set the book down and grabbed another one. He'd spent the better part of an hour getting them in chronological order, the best he could.

"Yes, but none of them are in Broken Bow, and I don't want to ship them out somewhere, letting people I don't know ready about my family before I get to learn all their secrets. I mean, come on, Gene. Would you want some stranger to know all about your family history and dirt before you found out? No. I don't think so."

Gene sighed. She was right, but he wouldn't say anything about it. He'd be a good boyfriend and do as she asked.

Boyfriend.

He rolled the word around in his head for a moment.

It still didn't fit right.

What was he?

Her lover?

Yes.

Her protector?

Yes.

Her baby-daddy?

Yes.

Gene wanted more.

What was *more*?

Marriage had always been something akin to a legal piece of paper, but really, that was it.

He needed more than simply a legal binding contract.

He wanted to be her soulmate.

"Gene," Jessica called him back to reality. "Don't you agree?"

"Oh, yeah. I guess so. Let me find that first book again."

With a cold beer on the table and a stack of journals beside him, he joined her on the couch and began reading.

The first journal was from 1895. Teenage Judith Sterry had received the first one from her mother as a gift and she documented the beginning of her relationship with George.

Aside from the end of the century speech, it sounded just like any other eighteen-year-old girl's diary. Full of odds and ends, romance, and home life.

Gene tried not to laugh when he caught Jessica blushing over an entry he was reading about the dating life of her great-great-grandmother. He'd never really had girls around him growing up, and didn't know how much of what he read was blush-worthy. However, he enjoyed the flush of color to his woman's cheeks.

Jessica didn't seem to add much to her computer files while he read. Just the occasional ticking of the keyboard when he'd stop to take a drink of his beer.

The 1895 journal ended with the year.

"Christmas has come and gone, and the new year is looming. Momma bought me more journals for the holidays. She said I need to document my entire life, as I will never know when I will need to look back on something. She's always a little on the different side. Daddy and George have been working together to get things ready for the wedding in the spring. Daddy's gonna turn the barn into a wedding pavilion. It's going to be a beautiful May wedding. I cannot wait for spring to come."

Gene polished off the last of his warm beer and got off the couch, headed toward the kitchen with the empty bottle in hand.

"Honey, can you grab me a ginger ale while you're in there?" Her sweet voice followed him through the house.

What a normal thing to be doing. Getting a beer and a soda for his pregnant girl.

When he stepped into the kitchen, Gene caught his reflection in the window's glass. Even though it was bright outside, he could see himself clearly, standing there like any other normal man.

Am I sure this isn't a dream?

Can this really be happening?

Maybe I'm trapped somewhere by something I should kill, but I don't want to let this go.

"Can you put it in a glass with some ice?" Jessica's voice once again brought him back to the moment.

"Yeah, babe. Got it." He shook his head to clear the fog and moved to the fridge and his goal.

Cold drinks.

"I've got the next journal ready. I'm hoping we can get through a few more before lunch," she continued talking from the other room. "But after this one, I think we should stop long enough to eat. Don't you think?"

Returning to her side, handing her the drink, Gene leaned down and kissed Jessica's forehead. "Maybe I should feed you first? I'd hate for us to get knee deep, and baby decided he's hungry."

As if on cue, her stomach made a grumble that would make a fat kid in a candy store proud.

"I think that is my answer." He laughed. "How about some sandwiches and potato chips?" He didn't wait for her to reply, just turned on his heels and headed back to the kitchen for food.

"June 21th, 1896. It is finally happening. I will become Mrs. George Ferguson today! The spring rains lasted far too long this year, putting everything off schedule. Including my wedding. But Momma says to have patience. Everything that should happen, will. Sometimes it just takes time. Momma says some of the most unusual things sometimes. But she's Momma, and I have become acquainted with her differences."

"Do you think there is something to her mom's madness?" Jessica asked. "Great Aunt Marge was a little different, too. Maybe dementia or some other mental disorder runs in my family."

"Just crazy, I think."

"Gene Benjamin Priest! I hope you are not calling me crazy!"

He laughed. The sound of her chastising him with his full name brought him a joy he never would've imagined. He couldn't explain why. It just did.

"I think there is something to it, but not the typical mental illness. Let's keep reading and see what else there is."

Nothing else in the second journal had them contemplating her family.

Jessica continued to type here and there, dates, and basic information following his reading. But when they moved into the journal labeled 1901, things changed.

The following year, the journals switched from being written by Judith to only seeing George's handwriting.

At this point, the family had welcomed Edith, and both of Judith's parents had been lost to pneumonia, only months apart.

Judith had assumed ownership of the family farm, a rarity for the time, but her father's will explicitly stated that it would be passed down only to the daughters of his lineage. George was very proud of his wife, and his father-in-law, for being so forward-thinking.

Gene came across a passage he'd read earlier, but continued on, now that they were at that point of fully reading through them.

"February 27th, 1901. Judith gave birth to a baby girl last week—sickly little thing. I don't think she will make it to the spring. Winter babies rarely do. Judith is adamant she will survive. We've named her Barbara, after my mother."

He continued.

"March 7th, 1901. We thought we lost our little Bobbie last night. She stopped breathing. I was in a panic. Judith wrapped her tightly in a blanket and took her into the dark of the night. Judith insisted her mother taught her a remedy from their European heritage, and the cold air of the night would help our darling babe. She stayed out with her all night, both so cold they were almost blue when they finally returned when the sun came up. Within hours of returning home, and with the heat of the hearth, Bobbie began wailing again. Her color has returned, and she is suckling. I have told my dearest Judith that this will be our last child. I cannot see my family suffer like this again."

. . .

"Who ever heard of taking a sick baby out into the cold?" Jessica exclaimed. "She could've killed her baby! I swear, they were so stupid back then!" She began typing aggressively on her laptop.

"Should we stop?" Gene asked.

"*No!*" She took a deep breath, then expelled it slowly. "Sorry. I shouldn't have yelled. That just made my blood boil. At least we know Barbara *did* survive and became a mom herself. It's just heartbreaking that her son died. But we will get to that later."

"Maybe we should stop there. We have over fifty of these to get through, but we have forever to get through them."

"Forever?"

Gene couldn't help but hear the joy in her voice at that simple word. Did they really have forever?

Most days, he was curious if he'd make it through the week. He'd never thought about long-term in any capacity.

This was foreign to him.

He could only nod at his woman, unable to form words, afraid anything he said would bring reality crashing down.

Gene didn't want to say anything that could bring her pain.

Jessica's phone rang, a song by her favorite pop band. *The Razor's Edge* diddy saved him from saying anything further.

CHAPTER
TWENTY-NINE

CHAPTER TWENTY-NINE

Tom

Tom went back into the bedroom from the en suite bathroom. The sight of the bed made, and a tuxedo laid out, took him aback.

What could we be going to that would require me to wear a tux?

He was just tucking his white shirt into his black slacks when Alex walked back into the room.

"Wow! You look sharp! Are you almost ready?" she asked. She'd changed into an early 50s-style pink dress. The ruching around the waist and bust accented her womanly figure. She'd pinned her hair up in curls on either side of her head.

His jaw dropped. She was so damn gorgeous.

"Tom, what's wrong?"

"You look amazing!"

She touched her cheek and blushed an appealing crimson. "Thank you. Where did that come from?"

He stepped over to her and pulled her into his arms. "I've

always thought you were beautiful. Forgive me if I don't tell you that enough."

She reached up and kissed him softly, then wiped the pink lipstick from his lips.

"Mommy?" a little voice said from behind her.

A little girl, about four years old, stood in the doorway. She had thick, dark brown hair that was up in pigtails and tied with sage green ribbons. Her dress was a similar color pink to Alex's, but it was sleeveless with a full skirt that came down past her knees and had a sage green sash tied around the waist.

"Samantha, come to show Daddy your pretty dress," Alex said, beckoning the little girl into the room.

She dashed to Tom and held up her arms to be picked up.

Tom picked her up and studied her little face.

She had his hazel eyes and Alex's dark hair.

How is this possible?

"We have a daughter?" he asked.

"Nope, just found this kid wandering around and thought, 'What the heck, let's bring her home'," Alex said sarcastically. Her expression seemed half-amused, but she had a delicate eyebrow arched as if she thought he was crazy.

Tom looked at the little girl in his arms again.

She was beautiful and even had a little dimple on her cheek, just like his.

"Her name is Samantha?"

"Tom, what happened on that hunt last night?" Alex asked, concern lacing her voice. "You asked me if we could name her after your mom as soon as we found out we were having a girl."

"You look so pretty," Tom said, his eyes tearing up. He nuzzled her warm little face.

"Don't cry, Daddy," she said, patting his cheek.

He chuckled.

"All right, you two, we gotta get going or we're going to be late." Alex headed out of the room, implying he should follow.

. . .

Alex drove them to a church that wasn't very far away.

Tom studied the building. It was an old-fashioned church with white wood siding and a steeple with a bell. There was a floral garland decorating the handrail on the three stairs leading up to the door.

Alex unbuckled Samantha from her car seat and set her on the sidewalk next to Tom.

"Come on, gotta get my basket," the little girl said, tugging on his hand.

Tom's mind raced. Why was he there?

He wore clothes that were too fancy, even for Easter.

Alex tucked her hand under his arm and started them in.

His heart hammered. When the doors to the entryway of the church opened, his eyes landed on Gene talking to Stacey.

His cousin was also in a tux and Stacey wore a sage green dress.

"Hey, you guys made it!" Gene said, striding over with a big smile on his face.

"Alex! Thank goodness you're here! I need your help." Stacey whisked Alex and Samantha away, leaving Tom alone with Gene.

"Gene, what the hell is going on?"

"We're having a wedding, Tommy!"

"That's not what I mean. I mean, I woke up in a house I'd never been to before to find out that Alex and I have a daughter. How the hell did that even happen?" Tom demanded.

"If you don't know how that happens, then I didn't do a very good job explaining things to you when we were younger." Gene laughed.

"No, I mean Alex can't have kids," Tom said.

A dark-haired little boy slammed into Gene's legs, pulling his cousin's attention away. Gene scooped him up in his arms. "Woah! Slow down, sport. What's the rush?"

"Benjamin Gilbert Priest! You get your butt back here!" Jessica yelled.

Tom and Gene both looked in the direction the boy had come from.

Jessica was waddling down the hall, one hand on her back to help balance her enormous, round belly.

"What did he do now?" Gene said, suddenly concerned instead of amused.

A knot formed in Tom's gut.

Gene had used that voice too many times on him.

"He is pulling apart the centerpieces I just finished putting together."

His cousin looked at the little boy in his arms. "Did you do what Mommy said?"

The boy shook his head.

"Benny, don't lie," Gene said in his dad voice.

"I just wanted to see," Benny said.

"All right, let's go clean up the mess so your mom doesn't have more work to do," Gene said, carrying the boy toward the reception hall.

What the hell was going on?

"You okay, Tom?" Jessica asked.

"No, I can't figure out what's going on."

She frowned. "What do you mean?"

"I mean, I can't remember any of this! I don't know how I got here or what's going on," he said, making tight fists at his sides.

"Take a deep breath," Jessica said calmly.

Tom obeyed, but it didn't clear his head.

"Let's just get through this wedding and then we can figure this out, all right."

Tom nodded.

"For now, I just need you to be an usher," Jessica said, walking him over to the door of the sanctuary. "Seat the guests of the bride here on the left, and guests of the groom on the right. Can you handle that?"

He smiled. "Yeah."

"I'll be back right before the ceremony starts." She headed down the hall where Alex and Stacey had gone.

Tom seated the guests and even recognized a few hunters who were attending. He still hadn't figured out who was getting married.

When Jessica returned, he seated her on the bride's side and sat beside her. He looked around for Gene and Alex. He didn't see either.

The music began and everyone twisted in their seats to watch.

A young man escorted Stacey down the aisle, and sat her in the front row, right in front of Tom. He then returned to the end of the aisle and escorted another woman forward and seated her across from them.

Tom figured it was his mother because he kissed her cheek, then went to stand by the minister.

The bridesmaids and groomsmen came down the aisle in pairs.

The young men in their early twenties, dressed in tuxedos with a beautiful young lady on each of their arms.

The girls all wore a sage green dress with a pink sash and carried bouquets of pink roses. When the last couple started down the aisle, Tom recognized the girl.

It was Sophie.

She was beautiful, her dark hair was elegantly pulled up, and she exuded femininity in pink.

When they had reached the front, Tom looked back and saw Alex with Samantha. The little girl had turned suddenly shy with all the eyes in the church on her.

Alex was kneeling down next to her, whispering to her and pointing down the aisle.

Tom twisted out of his seat and knelt in the aisle, beckoning her to him.

Alex smiled and whispered to the little girl again.

Samantha looked at him and ran down the aisle to him, throwing her arms around him and burying her face in his neck.

He smiled at Alex and sat back in his seat with Samantha in his lap. He wiped the tears from her cheeks and kissed the top of her head.

The music changed to the wedding march, and everyone stood, turning collectively to watch the bride come down the aisle.

Tears welled in his eyes as Gene escorted Chrissy down the aisle.

She was a vision in white. Her long blonde hair was in soft curls and crowned with a tiara and veil. She was smiling and happy as she looked at the man waiting for her at the end of the aisle.

The minister asked everyone to be seated as he began the ceremony.

Alex slipped into the seat next to Tom, and Gene went around to sit by Jessica.

He listened to the words of the ceremony, promising to love each other until death do they part.

Alex slipped her hand into his.

As he intertwined fingers with her, he lifted her hand to his lips and noticed the wedding ring on her finger.

It wasn't an enormous diamond, but just simple and elegant, just like Alex.

Tom sat contentedly with his wife next to him and their daughter in his arms.

CHAPTER
THIRTY

CHAPTER THIRTY

Alex

Alex stretched. Her back was stiff from sitting on the log trying to balance her computer. She checked the time. Tom had been gone for a couple of hours.

She couldn't detect any signs of him being hurt or in trouble, but a sense of unease washed over her, suggesting that something was wrong.

Alex wanted to call him but was afraid that if she did, it might alert the monster to his presence.

She set her computer down on the log next to the single earbud they'd found and walked back over to where she could see the foundry. Alex hoped she'd see him walking back toward her.

Of course, he wasn't.

There wasn't any sign of him.

Tom had told her to wait there. He'd also told Stacey he'd call if he needed help.

Alex didn't know what hunting experience Stacey had, but Gene would know what to do.

She dialed Jessica.

Tom might be mad later, but if it saved his life, he'd have to forgive her.

"Hey, Alex! Long time no chat," her bestie exclaimed.

"Hey, can I talk to Gene?" Alex asked.

"Geez! You've been gone almost a week, and you don't even want to talk to me? I'm hurt," Jessica teased.

"Jess, it's important. Can you just get him?"

"All right, hold on, he just stepped into the kitchen. What's going on?"

"I just have to ask a hunting question," Alex said.

"Gene? Alex's on the phone. She has a question for you."

"She sick of my cousin already?" Gene asked in the background. "I've got dish soap on my hands. Just put it on speaker. Hey, Alex, what's up?"

"I think Tom might be in trouble."

"What happened?" His voice was immediately sober.

"We're on a hunt and he hasn't come back," Alex said.

"What do you mean, you're on a hunt? I thought you were at the depot."

"We were, but Stacey called and now Tom's looking for a Djinn."

"A Djinn? Where are you?" Gene asked.

"Sioux City. I don't know what to do," Alex said, embarrassment eating her alive.

"Stay where you are, and call Stacey. I don't want you to be there alone. I'm on my way. I'll call you when I'm close and you can show me where Tom went."

"All right. Thank you, Gene."

The line went dead.

Alex paced across the path. She checked the GPS on her phone and put in the farm address.

Four hours! What if he doesn't have that long?

Tom's going to be mad that I called Gene.

She dialed the Sheriff's Office.

"Sheriff Martin, here," Stacey responded when the call was transferred to her.

"Stacey, it's Alex."

"What can I do for you, Alex?"

"Tom went to go check out the foundry, and he hasn't come back yet. I don't know what to do."

"How long has he been gone?"

"A couple of hours."

"Well, I wouldn't worry just yet. Sometimes it takes a while for those monsters to come out of the woodwork so they can kill 'em."

"Maybe..." Alex said, "I just thought he'd be back by now. He said he was just going to go see if he could find the nest."

"I'll cruise by out there and see if I can see anything. You sit tight and I'll get back to you."

"Thanks, Stacey." She hung up.

She looked around again while she waited for help to arrive. Alex couldn't just sit there if Tom was in trouble.

She started down the path, grateful she'd worn jeans and tennis shoes rather than a dress and heels.

Alex carefully approached the foundry.

Aging had caused many of the boards on the windows and doors to fall off, even though someone had boarded up most of them.

She found a window with a few missing boards. It was higher than she'd first assessed when she approached it, so she stepped up onto an old wooden crate that was under the window. Alex peered in, trying to see through the dirt.

There was a movement, and she tried to focus. She reached up and rubbed a spot clean with her hand and looked again. She hoped it was Tom, but the man was bald and had blue tattoos all over his head and hands.

She stretched up for a better look. When her weight transferred to her toes, the old weathered box gave out, and she fell with a crash.

Her foot got caught in the box, twisting as she landed on the side of it.

Alex stifled the cry of pain. She had to get away before the Djinn came to see what the noise was.

She pulled the box off her foot and tried to stand. Pain shot up her leg, and she quickly transferred her weight to the other leg.

A growl made her freeze.

Alex turned slowly, and the Djinn rushed toward her.

His blue eyes were illuminating, with no pupils, and the tattoos on his skin were glowing.

Alex tried to back up but stumbled on her damaged ankle. She fell backward onto her butt and scooted away, but he was on top of her before she could get more than a few feet from him.

He grabbed her and pulled her to her feet, and dragged her inside.

Alex fought him. She pulled and punched and scratched.

He punched her in the face and ribs a few times before finally picking her up and throwing her over his shoulder.

She kicked and pounded on his back, but he didn't seem to notice.

The Djinn dumped her on the ground inside the loading dock.

Alex looked around.

Tom was chained to a post along with four other victims.

She tried to get to him, but the Djinn had grabbed some rope and bound her hands.

She screamed in pain when he tied her feet together.

He left her lying on the dirty concrete floor.

"Tom! Tom, wake up!" she cried.

Her love just sat with his back against the post, his head lolling forward.

There was an IV tube running from his neck to a collection jar, but it wasn't blood that was draining.

The monster moved toward her with a metal pipe in his hand.

Alex screamed Tom's name as he swung the pipe at her.

Then everything went black.

*Jessica

Jessica looked down at her phone. "How far is it to Sioux City?"

"From here? About four hours, but I'll make it there sooner than that," he said.

"All right, let me throw some stuff in a bag really quick." She started for the stairs.

"You aren't going," he barked.

"The hell I'm not. Tom's in trouble and you know damn well that Alex isn't going to sit around and wait four hours for us to get there. So that means she might be in trouble, too. I'm going. Grab a few journals for me, will you? Four hours is a lot of reading time."

He huffed. "This was a battle I'm not going to win, isn't it?"

She nodded.

"Jessica, I swear, you are as stubborn as I am. Our kid is gonna be trouble."

He dried off his hands, leaving the rest of the dirty dishes for another time.

They were about an hour outside of Sioux Falls when Gene's phone rang. He put it on speaker.

"Hello?"

"Hey, Gene, it's Stacey. I asked Tom to come up and check out some disappearances and now I can't find him," she said.

"I'm already on my way," Gene said.

"How did you know?" Stacey asked.

"Alex called me a couple of hours ago."

"I can't find her either. I've checked all around the foundry, but didn't want to venture in there without backup."

"I'll be there shortly. Where should I meet you?" Gene asked.

Stacey gave him directions to the park, where she said she'd found Alex's truck.

The Mustang kicked up dust as Gene slid into the spot next to the truck.

A uniformed female sheriff was leaning against her SUV, waiting for them when they pulled in.

Gene and Jessica climbed out of the car.

"All right, give me the lowdown." He cut right to the chase.

The other woman looked at Jessica curiously, then back to Gene.

"Oh yeah right, Um...Stacey, this is Jessica. She's my...girlfriend."

She bit back her gasp. She didn't want Gene or the sheriff to see her pleasure or surprise. They hadn't ever really talked about it.

Stacey smiled approvingly. "It's about time you guys found a little happiness."

"Yeah, so tell me what you know," Gene said, getting back to business.

"Well, I drove around the foundry and saw nothing out of the ordinary. Tom had said that they wanted to check out Herb's camp too, so I drove over here and found the truck." The sheriff started walking into the park. "I came in here to see if I could find him and found this." She pointed to the small laptop and an earbud on the log.

"That looks like Alex's laptop," Jessica said. She wasn't about to let pregnancy slow her down a bit. She picked up the computer and opened it. The picture on the screen was a selfie of Alex and Tom. "It is Alex's."

"You know her?" Stacey asked.

"Yeah, she's my best friend."

Gene looked down the path to where the foundry stood. "Tom's in there and probably Alex, too. This is why you don't bring rookies on a hunt." He huffed and headed back to the Mustang. He popped the trunk and pulled out a long silver dagger. He then opened a small green cooler and brought out a jar. He dipped the blade into the thick red liquid.

"What's that?" Jessica asked, half-fascinated and half-repulsed.

"Lamb's blood."

She swallowed and stepped back. Her morning sickness had mostly subsided, but this was making her stomach turn.

Gene closed the trunk and started stalking toward the foundry.

Jessica and Stacey both started following him.

Gene stopped. "You are not coming."

Her face burned with anger. "Yes, I am." It was the Wendigo's cave all over again. He was ordering her around.

"No, you're not!" he commanded.

"That's my friend out there and I'm not leaving her."

"And I'm not risking the life of our child so you can play hero." His face was red, and his glare could kill.

Stacey's eyebrows shot up, and her eyes flashed to Jessica's belly. "I don't know how I missed the little bump there. Yours?" She blinked, looking from Gene to Jessica and back.

"Obviously," he drawled, before turning back to Jessica. "This demon will suck the soul right out of you and as much as you're willing to risk that, I"m not!" Gene said with finality.

Stacey stepped closer.

Jessica's gut said the sheriff would try to diffuse the situation.

"Gene's right, honey. You should wait here. I'll keep an eye on him, and we'll find Tom and Alex." She smiled. "You need to stay safe."

She frowned and growled to herself. They were probably right, but she would never admit that. However, she didn't want to risk her baby, she just needed Alex to be okay.

She grudgingly turned and stormed back to the car.

She didn't miss Gene, looking at Stacey and rolling his eyes, then heading toward the foundry, Stacey on his heels.

Jessica glared. She would yell at him for that later.

CHAPTER
THIRTY-ONE

CHAPTER THIRTY-ONE

Tom

Exhaustion threatened to eat him alive. This day had been the longest, most wonderful day he'd ever had. After the wedding, there'd been a reception, and he'd alternated dancing with Alex and keeping Samantha and Benny out of trouble.

It was so…normal.

Samantha had fallen asleep in the car on the way home and Alex had told him to go relax while she put their daughter to bed.

Tom slipped off his jacket and folded the shoulders together before tossing it on the foot of the bed. He sat on the end of the bed and slipped his shoes off. He stretched his sore toes. He wasn't used to wearing tight dress shoes for long periods of time.

He smiled as he replayed the day in his head, but something still didn't feel right.

Almost like it was too perfect.

Tom tried to recall the day before, but couldn't remember anything. In fact, he couldn't picture his *own* wedding day or the day his daughter was born. Important memories like those should be able to be pinpointed.

He lay back on the bed, his feet still touching the floor. His head was throbbing from thinking about all this.

Tom closed his eyes.

"Tom! Tom, wake up!"

Alex was calling him, and then she screamed.

When he opened his eyes, Tom was no longer in the bedroom, but in some sort of loading dock. He tried to move but his wrists were handcuffed with a chain that ran behind the pole he was leaning against.

He glanced around the dim room. There were others on either side of him, also chained to posts, and there was someone lying on the floor.

Alex.

Her hands and feet were bound with rope, and blood streamed down the side of her face. She was unconscious, but still struggling against her bonds.

Something moved in the dark and came for him.

A hand reached for his face and pain shot through him again.

"Alex!" He cried.

"Tom! Tom, what is it?" Alex asked, walking shaking him awake.

He sat up, breathing hard. He was in their bedroom. "I guess I dozed off."

Alex smiled. "Well, it was a busy day, and you got very little sleep last night. Would you mind?" she asked, turning and pointing at her zipper. She'd pulled all the pins out of her hair, leaving it in a riot of soft brown curls that bounced around her shoulders.

Tom reached up and slid the zipper down. He smiled as the back opened to reveal her lusciously tan skin and pink satin bra and panties.

Alex bit her lower lip as she turned, letting the dress slip from her shoulders.

. . .

Gene

Gene slid around the dilapidated building and found the spot Tom had to have entered. He signaled for Stacey to wait as he slipped quietly inside.

He quickly located where Tom and the others were being held.

There was a movement across a doorway in a back room. It had to be the Djinn.

Gene picked up a small piece of metal from the floor and threw it across the loading dock.

It landed with a clatter, and he ducked behind the metal shelving.

He watched through some stacks of old metal pieces as the Djinn emerged from a side room, heading toward the noise. Gray skin covered with navy blue tattoos of symbolic nature was the Djinn's normal appearance. Although the blue turned luminescent at times, along with the eyes. This male looked like it had been in a catfight. Scratches covered the creature's face and arms, and his eye was blackened.

Gene could only suppose either Tom or Alex did that to him.

The creature stepped closer to the metal Gene had thrown, and before he could lean down to inspect it, Gene rushed him.

The Djinn turned, catching him by the throat with one hand, and grabbing his wrist, the one that held the blade, with the other, lifting him off the ground. He squeezed Gene so hard it was either drop the blade, or lose the hand.

The blade hit the ground with a resounding *thud.*

Gene grasped at the hand around his throat, trying to break the grip that was cutting off his air. Stars were filling his eyes and he knew he had seconds to get away. Using the last fight tactic he liked to utilize, he thought it a *girly* movement, Gene brought his knee up hard into the male's anatomy.

The creature dropped to his knees, grasping his manhood, after letting Gene go.

Coughing hard, Gene tried to fill his lungs as the Djinn stood back up, his tattoos started illuminating.

This wasn't good.

When the Djinn used their 'gifts', their markings would glow before they attacked with a poison that would incapacitate their victims. No doubt this had happened to his cousin. He couldn't let it get him.

Gene rolled to the side, grabbing the blade that was still on the ground. Getting into a crouching position, he was ready.

"Let's dance," he teased the Djinn, waving for the creature to come his way.

The Djinn roared in anger and charged him.

Like a well-orchestrated dance, they fought enough other, a solid punch here, a slam against the wall there.

Gene threw his shoulder into the belly of the creature, wrapped his free arm around it, and slammed the tattooed beast to the ground before he drove the knife through its heart, twisting it in place.

The creature screamed as it denigrated into dust.

Gene grabbed the knife from the dusty pile and headed to where Tom and four other victims were bound.

They were all unconscious and chained to the pillars that held up the ceiling, while an IV attached to their necks drew blood out of them.

Gene pulled the IV out of Tom. He worked on removing the cuffs.

"Gene! Behind you!" Alex yelled.

It was too late.

Someone pounced on Gene from behind, biting into his neck.

He reached for the attacker and flipped them over his shoulder.

The figure landed on their back with a *thud*.

Gene wiped the blood from his neck and frowned at the creature in front of him.

It was a second Djinn.

How?

Everything he'd read about Djinn said they were solitary creatures. This one was female.

Maybe they were a mated pair?

She rolled over and pushed to her knees. She sprang at him again, screaming a guttural sound that would send chills down the spine of the average person.

She clawed at Gene's face.

He sucked in a breath at the sting his face endured as he threw her back.

The female landed on her feet like a cat, attacking him again with quick succession, clawing and moving back, always just out of his reach.

Gene waited for half a heartbeat, knowing she was about to launch again. The moment she charged at him, he dropped to one knee, slicing at her ankle, causing her to stumble.

He practically jumped on her, pinning her arms to the ground with his knees. Gene drove the knife into her chest.

The creature joined its mate in an ashen pile.

He picked up the blade and wiped it clean on his jeans.

Gene glanced around for Alex. He hadn't seen her when he entered the room.

She was on the floor in a dark corner. She was dirty and bleeding but looked all right, as far as he could tell.

"Are there any more?" he asked.

She shook her head. "Help Tom first. I'm okay."

"We'll need some help with the other victims." Gene stuck his head out the door and called Stacey, then went back to trying to free Tom.

"The key," Alex said. She pointed to a hook in the corner.

Gene grabbed it and unlocked Tom as Stacey entered the room with her gun drawn.

The sheriff quickly assessed the scene and holstered her weapon.

"Tom, Tom, wake up!" He slapped his cousin's face gently, trying to get him to wake up. "Pull the IVs out of the others," Gene told Stacey. "Come on, Tom, wake up!"

Tom's eyes slowly opened. "Gene?"

"Hey, easy now." He unlocked the other cuff.

The Djinn had drained his cousin severely because Tom didn't move.

There was no way Tom wouldn't demand to check on Alex if he could, but perhaps he didn't realize she was here.

"Come on, Tommy, let's get you out of here," Gene said, pulling the taller man to his feet.

His cousin leaned heavily on him as they moved toward the exit. As they neared Alex, Tom said her name.

It came out as a hoarse, scratchy sound.

"She'll be alright. I'll come right back for her if Stacey doesn't get her first," Gene said. He needed Tom to remain calm, so he didn't waste any more energy.

Jessica

Jessica stormed back to the Mustang; her face heated with anger. Although Gene was right, she wasn't used to being left out of the action.

The car door squeaked when she yanked it open. The journals were sitting on the backseat where she'd left them.

She'd scanned through the pages, reading the day-to-day happenings in her ancestors' lives. Nothing wild and crazy had been in the two journals she'd read on the drive up.

Now she needed a distraction.

Sitting alone in Gene's car wasn't helping her mood. His scent was all around her and she was still upset he wouldn't let her go with him.

Grabbing two more journals, Jessica shut the car door and moved over to see if Alex's truck was unlocked.

Jessica found that not only was it unlocked, but the keys were in it. She turned on the radio and smiled when country music started playing.

It was Alex's default. It always cheered her up.

She opened the first of the two journals. She couldn't guess how long Gene would be.

Jessica gasped. This journal was much more recent than the others. She recognized Great Aunt Marge's handwriting.

"August 30th, 1997. My sister, Beatrice, came to visit this week. She brought her husband and daughter. Said she wanted them to see where the magic came from. Alan is a good man. I can see how much he loves my baby sister. He is intelligent and could converse with me for hours. But that daughter of theirs. Jenifer is a handful. At eighteen, she should be more mature. All she wants to do is sit in the guest room and stare at herself in the mirror. Grams disapproves. She says a lady doesn't need to be painted up..."

She laughed. Her mother hadn't changed. Her mother had given her her love of makeup. Jessica wouldn't leave the upstairs unless she had on her face. She'd always say, "You never know who might stop by for a visit." Jessica flipped through a few more pages, skimming over the day-to-day life her great-aunt had lived. One entry really got to her.

"June 22nd, 1998. Beatrice was here. With Jenifer and her new baby, Emily Jessica. The babe isn't doing well. Jenifer said the doctors could not figure out what was wrong with her. My sister insisted she bring the infant to the farm. She thinks there are healing properties here. Aunt

Bobbie used to tell the story of how her life was saved when she was a babe, by something here. And they all call me crazy! But sure enough, Bea took that girl out one night and didn't return until morning. The gray skin of the baby had turned a beautiful pink color. And instead of crying, she was cooing. I know what they did but Grams says not to write about it—h"

Jessica jumped when her phone rang. She scrambled to answer. "Did you find them?" she said into the speaker. Her heart rebounded in her ears.

"Yeah, we found them. They're going to be all right. We need to get them to the hospital, though, so I'm heading up to get you as soon as Stacey and I release all the prisoners."

"How many are there?"

"Six, including Tom and Alex. I need to get the Mustang to get them to the Hospital."

"Alex left the keys in her truck. Would it be easier if I come to you?"

"Yeah. Her truck will hold more people. I'll see you in a minute," Gene said and hung up.

Jessica harrumphed. He hadn't even thanked her. She tossed the journal to the seat and put the truck in gear.

**Gene*

Gene pocketed his cell and whirled back into the building.

Tom grabbed his pant leg. "Please, help Alex," his cousin pleaded.

"That's what I'm doing. What were you thinking, bringing her on a hunt?" He didn't have time for the argument, but the words flew out of his mouth.

"I didn't bring her here. She must've followed me after I left her in the truck. It was going to be a quick recon before I took her back to the motel. I had every intention of coming back alone to kill the Djinn."

"You should've left her at the depot."

"I didn't mean for her to get hurt, Gene," Tom barked.

"You should've called me *before*. Like when Stacey reached out. I could've met you here and then neither of you would've gotten hurt." He shook his head. He could get onto Tom more later; he did need to save his girl's best friend.

Stacey was pulling the IVs from the victims.

Despite the stripper being beyond saving, Herb, the young girl, and the unidentified new guy were still alive.

The sheriff hadn't untied Alex. He went to his cousin's woman, pulling out his pocketknife.

"Oh, I didn't even see you there, Alex," Stacey said.

"It's okay. It's more important for you to help them," Alex said.

Gene cut her bonds and pulled her to her feet, then went to help Stacey.

They uncuffed all the people, then helped them outside, Tom among them.

"Where's Alex?" Tom asked, his voice full of panic, and frantically scanning the area behind them as he sat on a large rock outside.

"She's still inside with Herb, he's too weak to stand, and she didn't want him to be alone," Stacey said. "She's okay, Tom."

Tom tried to get up, but he slid back down to his butt.

Stacey steadied him. "I think you'd better wait here."

Jessica pulled into the parking lot in front of the foundry.

Gene guided her to park as close as she could to the rock.

She jumped out of the truck and ran over to his cousin. "Tom, are you all right?" Her brow was tight with concern.

"Yeah, I'm fine."

"I know you're lying, but I really didn't expect any other answer from you," Jessica smirked.

"Where's everyone?" Tom asked.

Gene put a hand on his cousin's shoulder. "Stacey and I have a few more people to bring out. They're too weak to walk on their own. Just stay here with Jessica and keep her safe."

Tom couldn't hold up an ink pen right now, let alone keep his woman safe, but he had to give his cousin something to hold on to so he wouldn't try to be the hero again.

Jessica walked over to Gene and Stacey when they emerged from the foundry, one on each side of an old man who was too weak to walk. "Where's Alex?"

"She's right behind us," Gene said as if that should be obvious. He glanced over his shoulder, but she wasn't there.

Jessica flashed a disapproving look and walked into the foundry, Gene right on her heels.

He'd left Herb with Stacey because there was no way his woman was going into the foundry alone, even though the Djinn were dead.

They ran into Alex trying to make her way across the factory floor limping. There was blood running down the side of her face from a cut on her head.

Gene winced. He hadn't known she was hurt.

"Oh my God! Alex, are you okay?" Jessica demanded, rushing to her.

"Yeah, I'm fine. Stupid Djinn just whacked me over the head."

"It didn't feed off you?" Gene arched an eyebrow.

"The male wanted to, but the female wouldn't let him. They seemed to argue over it in some language I didn't understand," Alex said, frowning.

"Wait! There were two of them?" Jessica gaped.

"Yeah, I think that's how they got to Tom. He was only expecting one," Gene said. "We've never heard of two of them nesting together."

When they got back outside, Stacey and Tom were helping the victims in the truck.

They put the three of them in the backseat.

His cousin climbed into the bed of the truck.

"Alex, you ride up front with Jessica and she can drop us at our cars before heading to the hospital," Gene said.

Alex nodded and obeyed, while Gene and Stacey got in the bed with Tom.

Jessica drove extra cautiously, likely to prevent the victims from being injured any more than they already were.

CHAPTER
THIRTY-TWO

CHAPTER THIRTY-TWO

Tom

It was getting late, and Tom pulled on his flannel to leave his exam room. They'd been trying to replace the fluids he'd lost. He was lucky, though; the others were all admitted, and they weren't sure if the homeless guy was going to make it.

He approached the nurses' desk to find out where Alex was.

They directed him to a room just around the corner.

When their gazes met, Alex audibly swallowed, as if she was afraid of him. Her expression was stamped with trepidation.

"Alex, are you okay?" Tom frowned. He didn't want to step closer and scare her more.

"I'm sorry, Tom. Please don't be mad at me," she said, tears welling up in her eyes.

He dashed to the side of the bed. "Why would I be mad at you?"

"'Cause I called Gene." Tears streamed down her cheeks.

Tom let out a breath. He sat on the side of her bed. "I'm not mad at you."

"But you said not to call Gene."

He sighed. He hated being in his cousin's shadow, but Gene always had his back. "Alex, you saved us all," he admitted.

"I was so scared," she whimpered. "I couldn't lose you again."

Tom pulled her into his arms. He held her to him, feeling the relief of just having her close to him. His mind drifted to the dream he'd had of them while in the djinn's lair. He longed for it to come true, but it was impossible. He couldn't tell her about it, either, because he didn't want her to feel bad that she couldn't have kids. It wasn't Alex's fault.

"Tom, what's wrong?"

He pulled away and wiped away the tears he couldn't stop. "It's nothing. I'm just glad you're safe."

The stern look on Alex's face said what her lack of words couldn't. She didn't believe him, but the doctor came in before she challenged him.

"Well, it's not broken, so that's the good news," the doctor said.

"What's not broken?" Tom asked, standing to face the doctor.

"My ankle," she said.

"It's a severe sprain and can still take a few weeks to heal, so you'll need to stay off it as long as possible."

"I'll make sure she does," Tom said.

"All right, the nurse is going to bring you in a brace and you will want to get some crutches. I'm going to write out a prescription for some pain meds and you should be ready to go." The doctor smiled and excused himself.

Tom pushed Alex's wheelchair to the lobby, where they met Gene and Jessica.

"Back to the motel?" his cousin asked.

"I need to pick up Alex's prescription," he said.

"We could all use some food, too," Jessica said. "Tom, why don't you come with me, I can drop you off to get the script, and

I'll get some food and pick you back up. Gene can drive Alex back to the motel and get a room for us."

"Okay." Tom nodded.

They headed out to Alex's truck while Gene pulled the Mustang up to the front door to pick up Alex.

Gene

"Thank you for giving me a ride," Alex said, trying to break the awkward silence.

Gene had barely spoken to her—or Tom—since he'd rescued them. He had too much to say, but couldn't find the words. The whole thing was just so odd.

"Well, Jessica asked me to, and it's not like you could climb up in that truck anyway," he huffed.

"Thank you for saving Tom," she whispered.

He shot her a glance. She hadn't said saving *them*, just Tom.

Of course, he would always save Tom. He'd die for his cousin. It was his job to protect the man who was more like a brother than a cousin.

"I shouldn't have had to rescue Tom. I should've been with him from the beginning, but since Tom decided to impress you with his hunting skills, he almost got you both killed," Gene growled at her. He was being an asshole, but he wasn't sorry, and he couldn't help it.

"He wasn't trying to impress me," Alex snapped. "He was trying to stop the Djinn."

He arched an eyebrow. Almost admired her spunk. "Well, he should've called me and left you at home," Gene said, raising his voice.

Alex threw a glare. "If you want to be mad, fine be mad, but don't take it out on Tom. He was just trying to do his job. A job you taught him, by the way, and he doesn't deserve to have you looking down your nose at him all the time."

"Hey, he's the one who insisted on learning. He knew what kinda life this was. He walked in with his eyes open. We didn't have any problems until he met you," Gene barked.

Again, he wasn't going to apologize for being a jerk.

They pulled up to a stoplight and Alex got out of the car. She slammed the door and started hobbling toward the sidewalk.

Gene growled.

Why were women so frustrating?

She couldn't be part of their world—neither of the girls could.

"Alex, get back in the car!"

She ignored him and just kept walking.

Alex started down the side street to get away from him, but Gene pulled the Mustang around the corner and parked a bit in front of her.

He got out, slamming the door behind him, too.

Alex's ankle gave out, and she fell as he walked toward her.

He stood over her, but she didn't look up at him.

"Damn it Alex, what's wrong with you?"

Gene bent down on one knee to pick her up.

When she finally met his gaze, she was pale and covered in a sheen of sweat. Tears welled up in her eyes. "Don't you see? He idolizes you. I told him to take the truck and come get you, but he wanted you to have time with Jessica."

He reared back and swallowed. Words didn't happen when he tried to talk.

"He wants to make you proud and all you do is criticize him."

"I don't always criticize him." The venom he'd felt was gone, and guilt bit at him for yelling at her.

"Yes, you do! You blame him for what happened today, but how was he supposed to know there were two Djinn? Djinn lives alone, they don't travel in groups. Even you got surprised by one, Mr. High-and-Mighty!" Alex exclaimed.

Gene didn't want to admit it, but she was right. He had experienced being caught by a Djinn a couple of years ago, and he recalled how enticing that dream could be.

He let out an exasperated breath. "You're right," he mumbled.

"Excuse me?" Alex asked, her mouth half-hanging.

"You're right," he said a little louder. "Maybe I was too hard on him tonight."

"It's not his fault I was there, either. After I called you and Stacey, I went to see if I could find him. That stupid Djinn caught me outside the foundry when the box I was standing on collapsed and I twisted my ankle. I tried to fight him off, but he was too strong."

"So you're the reason the male Djinn was all scratched up," Gene said, lifting his chin. "But you still should've waited for me."

"Would you have waited?" she asked, her dark eyes glinting with a dare.

"That's different. I'm a trained hunter."

"But you'd do whatever it takes to save someone you love," Alex said, as if she knew him.

Of course, she was right, but he wasn't about to tell her that.

Gene studied the sincere look on her face. "You really love him, don't you?"

"With all my heart. I would die for him." Her chin was set, her mouth in a hard, serious line.

He pulled her into his arms, truly hugging her for the first time. "You love him as much as I do," he whispered above her ear.

She looked up at him. "I do."

"Come on, we better get you back to the motel before Tom and Jessica arrive or Jessica is gonna kick my ass."

Alex laughed as Gene scooped her up in his arms and carried her to the Mustang.

Tom

. . .

Tom opened the door to his motel room and set the prescription and truck keys on the table.

Jessica was right behind him, carrying the food.

Gene and Alex weren't there. They couldn't be far, because the Mustang was parked outside.

"Alex?" he called.

There was no answer, but he heard the shower was running.

Tom just opened the door to the bathroom and peeked behind the curtain. "What's going on here?" he teased.

Alex gasped and grabbed for the curtain to cover herself. She was alone, her body covered in soap. "Tom Priest! You scared the daylights out of me! What is wrong with you?"

"Sorry, I was just worried I'd lost you, again. Where's Gene?"

Alex paused and stared, shaking her head before answering. "I think he went to get him and Jessica a room."

Tom stared at her a moment, looking at the cut on her head, the black and blue her ankle was turning, and it hit him. "I can't do this," slipped from his lips. He turned and left the bathroom, shutting the door behind him.

Jessica was pulling food out of the brown paper bags, when the door to his room opened and Gene entered, carrying a bucket of ice and a key to his own room. "Good, you're here! I'm starving," his cousin said, as he set the bucket of ice down. He leaned over and kissed Jessica.

Tom made his way to the door and outside.

"What was that about?" Gene asked Jessica.

He heard his cousin speak before the door even closed.

"I don't know. I thought he just checked on Alex," Jessica said.

"Guess we'll ask Alex when she comes out."

Alex

. . .

Alex sat in the shower; her arms wrapped around her knees with the water pouring over her.

How could Tom not want her now?

Why would he say that after everything?

She thought she would be the one to break things off. Not him.

He was right, though.

This wasn't the life she wanted.

She knew she couldn't handle being at another hunt. But she also would not be alright waiting at home, hoping he was safe.

Maybe they should end things.

She cried until she had no more tears, then shut off the water.

Crawling out of the tub, Alex could still hear voices in the room, so she got dressed and sat on the small towel that she'd put on the floor. She towel-dried her hair and combed it out.

Listening carefully, she could hear the conversion on the other side of the paper-thin walls.

"Gene? Now that you have devoured that burger, why don't you go check out to our room and get the overnight bags from the trunk?"

"That sounds like a good idea, babe. I'll handle that now."

Still in a mood, Alex tried not to laugh at his obviousness.

Jessica had to have indicated without speaking, that she wanted it to be just them.

She heard the outside door open and close just seconds before Jessica knocked on the bathroom door.

"Alex, are you all right?" her bestie asked.

"I'm fine."

"Then why don't you come out? We have food."

"I just want to be alone," she said.

"The guys left. It's just us," Jessica said.

"Please go away."

"You know me better than that. I'm your best friend and I'm not leaving."

"You can't fix this."

"Fix what? What happened, Alex?" Jessica twisted the nob on the door but Alex had locked it.

"Just please go. I'll talk to you tomorrow, but I just can't right now," she pleaded.

"Only if you promise to talk to me tomorrow."

"I promise," Alex said, stifling a sob.

"Our room is three doors down if you need me," her bestie said. "No matter what time it is. I'm here for you."

"I know."

Alex waited until she was sure she was alone. She hobbled out of the bathroom, quickly packing her clothes and grabbing her keys off the table.

She was glad her truck was an automatic, and she only needed her right foot to drive.

Alex pulled out of the parking lot and headed for Nebraska. As she drove, she mentally packed what she needed from Jessica's house. The hard part would be loading the horses with her bad ankle.

CHAPTER
THIRTY-THREE

CHAPTER THIRTY-THREE

Tom

Tom walked down the street to clear his head. What had he been thinking? He had a bond with Alex that they both felt.

She hadn't meant to put herself in danger.

But this wouldn't be the last time he had to go on a hunt.

Could he really walk away from the hunter life?

He loved her.

And he would give it all up for her.

But seeing her hurt had been too much.

Now he'd screwed everything up, and she'd probably never speak to him again.

A bar came into view and the fantasy of a cold, stiff drink had Tom entering the establishment.

He had to figure out what to say to Alex, and it better be good. He wanted to share the dream he'd had while the Djinn had him, but he didn't want to hurt her since she'd said she couldn't have children.

He ran a hand over his face and ordered a bourbon. Double.

It'd started to rain when Tom made his way back to the motel. He had to make things right with Alex.

He couldn't lose her.

The lights were off when he entered the room. He quietly slipped over to the bed, so he didn't wake her. However, the bed remained made and Alex wasn't in it.

Tom flipped on the light. The room was empty and all of Alex's things were gone. He rushed to the window and scanned the parking lot. The truck was gone, too.

She'd left him.

He deserved it, but he couldn't let her go that easily.

Tom called her phone, but it rang through to voicemail. He hung up and called again. It went to voicemail again.

He grabbed his laptop and set it on the table.

Grateful for his technological abilities, he started up the computer to track her phone. A small white paper bag caught his attention, still sitting on the table.

Her prescription was still inside.

The morphine they'd given her at the hospital would've worn off by now and she'd be in pain.

Tom had to find her.

He loaded the tracking website and located her phone. She was only fifty miles west of Sioux City.

He dialed Gene.

"Tom? What's up?"

"Alex is gone."

"Gone? What do you mean, she's gone?" Gene asked.

"I mean, she took all her stuff and left it in her truck. I gotta go get her. She's only about an hour from here."

Tom overheard Gene telling Jessica what was happening.

"I can't just leave you here and she's got an hour head start on us," his cousin said.

Jessica's voice was loud enough for him to catch her response. "I'll be fine. I know you can catch her. Just come back to me when you find her. I'll try to call her and convince her to come back."

"All right, but don't leave this room. I'll be back soon," Gene said. "Meet you in the car," he said to Tom.

Tom threw his things in his bag and headed out to the Mustang.

Gene was already waiting in the driver's seat.

He tossed the bag In the back and climbed in.

"Where is she now?" his cousin asked.

"Her phone hasn't moved, so she may have stopped some-where to rest. Her pain meds are wearing off, so she won't be able to drive for long," Tom said.

"Which way?" Gene asked.

"West."

"She's heading to the farm."

"Yup. That'd be my guess," Tom said.

They pulled out and headed to the freeway.

"So, what did you dream about?" his cousin asked, when the silence had dragged out too long.

"What?"

"With the Djinn, they fulfill your deepest wish. So, what was it?" Gene asked.

His knee-jerk was to tell his cousin to go to hell; it was none of his business. Deep down, he admitted that was only because if he was honest, Gene would tell Jessica something Tom couldn't even tell the woman he loved.

"We were at Chrissy's wedding," Tom sighed as the truth flew out.

"Chrissy? Your deepest wish is to see Chrissy get married?" Gene threw him a surprised look.

"Not just that. You and Jessica were there with your son and Alex—h" he broke off, getting a little choked up.

"What about Alex?"

"She was helping our daughter be the flower girl."

Gene went silent.

It wasn't a shocker, what his cousin was thinking. He'd been thinking about it as well. After all, they'd been through, neither of them wanted to subject a child to their lifestyle, but now his cousin was about to.

Tom stared out the window, leaving his tale hanging in the night air.

"I thought you said she was only fifty miles from Sioux Falls?" Gene frowned.

"Yeah, we should be close," Tom said, looking around.

"There ain't nothing out here, Tommy. Are you sure you're looking at that right?"

He glanced at the screen again. The signal from his phone was quickly approaching the signal from hers, and yet they were miles from the next town.

Tom had a bad feeling something was wrong. He forced his eyes to scan the darkness, straining, so he didn't miss her. As they came to the truck turnout, he spotted the blue truck. "There!" He pointed.

Gene slammed on the brakes and swerved over behind the truck.

Tom jumped out before the car fully stopped. "Alex!" he called as he ran to the truck. He knocked on the window. She wasn't in the front, so looked in the back. "Alex, it's Tom," he pulled on the lever, and, to his surprise, it opened.

She was lying on the seat curled up in a ball, shivering. Her head was closest to him. He ran a hand over her wet hair. "Alex, wake up," he breathed.

She tilted her head up. "Tom?"

"Yes, honey, I'm here," he said, petting her hair again. "Why are you all wet?"

"I threw up outside and it was raining," Alex said through chattering teeth.

He pulled off his jacket and covered her with it. "I need to get you someplace warm."

"How'd you find me?"

"I tracked your phone."

Alex looked away. The redness in her cheeks was visible, even in the dimness of the truck lot.

Tom closed his eyes and took a deep breath. It wasn't a shocker that she was still mad, but he'd hoped coming to find her would make up for his lapse in judgment. "You rest. I'm going to grab my bag and we'll go home." He kissed her head and closed the door. He walked back to the Mustang and grabbed his bag out of the back.

"She okay?" Gene asked.

"I think so."

"Why'd she stop here?"

"She said she got sick," Tom said.

"Sick?"

"Yeah, I'd imagine from the pain. She didn't take her pain pills."

"What are you going to do?" his cousin asked.

"I'm going to take her back to the depot. I think that Djinn really messed with her head," he lied.

"All right. I gotta go back to Jessica. Call if you need us. We'll probably head back to the farm tomorrow."

"Thanks." Tom headed back to the truck as Gene pulled out.

Three hours later, Tom pulled the truck onto the dock of the depot.

Alex was still lying in the backseat.

He'd turned on the heater and driven in silence, hoping she'd sleep.

She'd told him she had a high pain threshold, and he imagined that was why she'd gotten sick.

They didn't speak, but words of wisdom didn't come into his head, anyway.

What could he say?

Of course, he owed her a giant apology.

Tom convinced himself he would deal with whatever was required when the time came. He loved her.

She loved him.

It would have to be okay.

He opened the back door to find Alex asleep. He hated to wake her, but she would be more comfortable in his bed. Tom slid his arms under her and pulled her to him.

She groaned in her sleep.

"Come on, sweetheart, let's go to bed," he breathed.

Alex wrapped her arms around him and rested her head on his shoulder.

Tom carried her inside, setting her down on the bed. Removing her wet pajamas, he put one of his clean T-shirts on her.

He covered her up and took a shower. He was exhausted and just wanted to sleep.

Tom crawled into bed beside Alex, laying on his side, watching her sleep. He wanted to hold her, but he didn't feel he had the right.

He'd messed up, and he'd be lucky if she forgave him.

Tom fell into a restless sleep, waking several times to check on Alex.

Gene

Gene slipped quietly back into the motel room. The light and TV were on but Jessica was asleep on the bed.

Her beautiful was hair fanned out across the pillow.

She was a sight to behold.

He undressed and turned out the light before slipping into bed next to her.

Jessica stirred, and her eye fluttered open. "Did you find her?" Her voice was full of sleep.

"Yeah, we did," he said, pulling her into his arms.

"Why did she leave?" she asked, snuggling against him.

Gene sighed, exhaustion looming over him. "I don't know. Tom said, the Djinn really messed with her."

Jessica rolled over to face him. "The Djinn didn't do anything to her." She frowned.

"What?" he asked, struggling to focus. All he wanted to do was sleep.

She propped up on her elbow. "Alex told me that the Djinn didn't put her in the trace to feed from her."

"That doesn't make sense," Gene said. "I cut her free of her bonds myself. She was bleeding."

"She said that the female wouldn't let the male touch her."

He frowned again and sighed. "Well, I guess you'll have to ask her about it tomorrow. I just want to sleep."

"But Gene—"

"Jessica, I'm exhausted. Can we just get some sleep and figure it out later? It doesn't matter. They are *both* safe, and Tom took her to the depot. It's all good." He didn't mean to snap, but he was beyond exhausted.

The sun was coming up, and he hadn't slept at all yet.

"I'm sorry. You need to rest," she whispered. "I just can't figure out why Alex had lied to Tom."

Gene pulled her tight against him and was out immediately.

CHAPTER THIRTY-FOUR

*Alex

Alex awoke several hours later. Where was she?

What time was it?

She was in a bed.

She sat up and looked around. Recognition hit. She was in Tom's room, in the depot.

Tom was asleep next to her, facing the opposite wall.

How had she gotten back here?

Her stomach lurched, and Alex swallowed. She almost puked right there.

She hobbled into the bathroom and threw up twice.

Tom followed her a couple of minutes later. "Are you okay?"

Tears stung her eyes.

He didn't love her anymore.

How could he?

He didn't trust her.

She'd gotten caught by the Djinn and they both almost died.

Tom knelt down next to her, rubbing his hand across her back. "What can I do for you?"

"Can you get my toothbrush out of my suitcase?" she asked, without looking at him.

Tom left the room, reemerging moments later with a brand-new toothbrush. He cracked open the package and put some toothpaste on it, then wet it and handed it to her.

Alex sat back on her butt, leaning against the wall. The floor was cold, and it felt good against her flushed skin. "This isn't mine."

"It is now. Your bag's still in the truck. This is new. I always keep new spares around. I never know when Gene is gonna do something stupid to mine. But I'll go to the truck and get your bag soon. I don't want to leave you right now."

She chose not to comment about his last statement and stuck the toothbrush in her mouth.

Tom felt her forehead. "You seem a little warm, and you're sweating? What can I do?"

"Nothing," Alex around the toothbrush. She needed to rinse her mouth and struggled to get up.

Tom pulled her up and kept a hand on either side of her waist while she rinsed. He then scooped her up and carried her back to the bed. He sat next to her, facing her.

"Please don't," she said, fighting tears. She didn't want him to see her cry.

"Don't what?"

"Be so nice to me. You don't trust me." Alex meant to bark the words, but they came out in a pained whisper.

"I do trust you. I don't know what got into me. Just the thought of you being hurt like that again, or worse..." Tom stood up and fell into a pace at the end of the bed.

"I didn't mean to get caught, Tom. It had been hours. I thought you might be dead. I couldn't sit around for four hours waiting for Gene. I get it, that you're mad. You have every right to be. If you don't want me around anymore, that's fine. If my truck is here, I'll just go."

"No, please, I'm so sorry. I don't know why the thought would even pop into my head, but I don't want to lose you," he pleaded.

Alex narrowed her eyes. He looked like he was in so much pain, and his heart ached. "What did you dream about, Tom?"

He stopped pacing and met her gaze. "What do you mean?"

"When you were under the spell of the Djinn, did you dream I was with Gene?"

"No, of course not!"

"Then what? That you never met me?"

"I don't remember." Tom's voice was flat, and she saw the lie for what it was.

Alex swallowed and nodded. She got up and started toward the door. Her ankle screamed, but she didn't care.

Tom stopped her. "Please don't go," he whispered, his plea barely audible.

"You haven't given me a reason to stay. You don't even trust me enough to tell me the truth."

"It's not that. I just didn't want to hurt you more," he said, sitting on the end of the bed.

"You can't hurt me more than you did last night."

Pain crossed his face. "I dreamt about you."

Alex frowned. "What about me?"

"That we were married, and we had a daughter."

Kids, I knew it.

"Her name was Samantha, named after my mom. She had your dark hair and my eyes."

Alex swallowed again, trying to hold back the tears. "I told you, I can't have kids."

"I know. That's why I didn't want to tell you."

She stepped back over to Tom; he slid to his knees in front of her and wrapped his arms around her, his head resting against her belly.

"I want you, and if that's all there will ever be, I'm okay with it always being just the two of us."

"Then why did you say 'I can't do this'?"

"I don't know. I came in, heard the shower and I saw all your injuries, your bared soul. The thought that I almost lost you, had me realizing I can't live without you. I won't let you be in danger like that again. Please forgive me. I was terrified."

She sighed. "I want you too. But if you don't trust me—"

"I *do* trust you. I know you didn't purposely put yourself in danger. You made all the right choices, calling Gene and Stacey."

Alex stepped away from him and sat on the bed. She was sweating again from the pain in her ankle. She took slow, deep breaths to calm the nausea.

"Are you okay?" Tom asked. "Can I get you something?"

"No, I just should've stayed off my ankle."

He stood and lifted her legs onto the bed. He grabbed his pillow and put it under her foot. "I'll get some ice and your pain pills." He disappeared through the door.

She closed her eyes.

He was terrified.

So scared of the thought of losing me.

No one has ever wanted me like that.

Tom returned with an ice pack, a bottle of pills, a glass of water, and some Ritz crackers. He set the ice gently on her ankle.

Alex sucked in a breath from the burst of cold.

Then he sat on the edge of the bed and handed her the water. Laying the crackers between them, he opened the pill bottle and handed her one.

She popped it in her mouth and drank half the glass of water with it.

He opened the crackers and held out the tube to her.

"I'm all right. Once the pain pill kicks in, I'll be fine," Alex said, waving off the crackers.

"You need something with that pill, or it will tear up your stomach," he insisted.

She took a few crackers. "Actually, I'm feeling a little better and I think I just need to eat something."

"What would you like?" Tom asked.

"Pancakes actually."

He smiled and kissed her forehead. "Pancakes it is then! You get comfortable and I'll get some food started." He headed for the door.

Alex checked her phone. He must've left it on the nightstand for her. It'd been in her pajama pants pocket and she could see the navy blue material with its moons and stars lying mixed with Tom's clothes on the floor. She smiled. She enjoyed seeing their things together.

Somehow, it was comforting.

Tom returned with more pillows and his laptop. He placed one pillow behind her, propped her up against the headboard, and tossed a couple of others on the other side of her for himself. "I thought you could find us a movie to watch while I fix us the pancakes."

Alex smiled as Tom left the room again. Suddenly, everything seemed right again.

CHAPTER THIRTY-FIVE

Gene

"You wouldn't believe what I just read," Jessica boomed to Gene from the library, while he was in the kitchen, fixing them lunch.

He'd never been a kitchen rat. That was usually his cousin's job. However, his woman had given him a reason to learn to create in the kitchen.

He stared at his masterpiece of a sandwich and laughed to himself.

Scooby and Shaggy would be proud.

"Will you come in here, so I don't have to scream," she hollered back.

"Just give me a moment," Gene said. "I'm coming with your lunch." He'd barely stepped into the room when she started ranting.

"So, get this. Remember how the family tree had Henry, um, Barbara's son, died at fifteen? This journal reads very differently."

He sat down beside her and took a big bite of his sandwich. "Whaph dubs it say?" he asked, his mouth still occupied.

"Please don't talk with your mouth full, honey. Makes me queasy."

He swallowed and followed it with a long pull from his bottle of beer. "My apologies. I will learn. What does it say that is so different?"

"This one is in Edith's handwriting. She took over journaling after her parent's deaths when the farm passed down to her."

"Damn. How many people in the family wrote in these?" he asked.

"From what I can tell, almost everyone that has lived here has written in them at one point or another."

"I guess I better buy you some books to keep up the family tradition."

Jessica rolled her eyes, then pointed to the journal.

"June 22, 1936. As the sun rose this morning, we said goodbye to my nephew, Henry. It's a bittersweet evening, this Litha. He reached his majority only forty-five days ago. We had fifteen wonderful years with him. Bobbie isn't taking it well. What mother would? Goodbyes are always hard. But he was a greater purpose, a higher calling, waiting for him on the other side. I know we will see him again."

"What is so weird about that? It sounds like they were having his funeral," Gene said. "They did things a little different from what we do now."

"Hold on, I'm not done," Jessica retorted. She flipped through a few pages before she picked up reading again.

"December 22, 1936. I saw Henry this afternoon, as the sun was at its furthest. He was standing by the tree where Daddy's buried. Momma

always said there was something magical there. It's where she took Bobbie as a baby when she almost died. I've never noticed anything special before. Until today. Henry has grown more. I'd say he is now as tall as Daddy was. His hair is longer, too. I called out to him, with no response. When I stepped closer, he faded away, like the mist of a memory. My dear Otto thinks I am seeing things. And I agreed. I saw my nephew."

She set the journal down to free her hands to enjoy a bite of her sandwich. She let out a contented sigh.

"So, I made a decent enough lunch? Is baby happy, too?"

"Gene, anything you make for me to eat makes the baby happy. It's nice to sit here and just read. You were right about that."

"I'm sorry, what?" he teased.

"You were right. I needed to read all the journals before trying to decide what was important, and what was just filler. Like these entries. What do you think?"

With his background, Gene knew better than to discount anyone's unusual situations. However, this simply reads like a grieving family.

There was nothing paranormal about the words his woman had read aloud.

"I'm more curious to hear what you think about that," he said.

"Well, only months ago, I thought it was impossible for a house to be haunted. And in a short amount of time, I have been exposed to ghosts, Wendigos, Djinns, a pregnancy. All things I never would've believed in. Do I think Edith saw her nephew? Yes, I do. Do I think he was a ghost? Maybe. What else could he be?"

"Hand me one of Marge's journals. I want to thumb through and see if your great aunt ever saw Henry." He slid into research mode, even though he wasn't hunting anything in particular. Not to mention, that was his cousin's gig.

Tom would be so proud of me. Research, ha!

He opened the caramel-colored leather journal his love handed over.

"June 24th, 1998. My sister and her daughter left, taking the baby with them. Beautiful Emily Jessica. I wish she could've stayed. Grams is glad they left. She says the family line skipped Jenifer, like it skipped Edith. She didn't want to be in her presence any longer. Said the woman sucked all the positive energy out of the air. We both wanted them to leave the baby here, but Jenifer wouldn't hear it. She needs to be here. The child can't learn about her heritage if she's not here. Grams promises to tell me more when the time comes. For now, I'll stay here, keep the farmstead ready for the day she comes back."

Gene looked up at Jessica, staring at her intensely. He tried to see her with fresh eyes. Or new information. There was something about the Ferguson family that wasn't entirely…normal.

Of course, I can't fall for a girl that's normal. No. I gotta fall for a preternatural offspring of… of what?

There'd been enough odd signs over the six months since they had met. Gene hadn't put them all together until now.

What is she?

Christmas was right around the corner, and Tom and Alex were coming to spend the week with them.

This was something he couldn't research on his own. Gene was too close, and worried he'd miss something, or go off a deep end and not find his way back.

Jessica was his heart. Their baby would be their world.

What if the baby was something more, too?

He needed to know how to care for it.

Gene let out a deep sigh.

"You okay?" Jessica asked.

"Yeah. I think we should put this away for now. We've got some decorating to do!"

"Decorating?"

"Christmas is next week, right? Tom and I haven't had a real Christmas since… since… You know, I can't remember."

"Oh! We better do something about that! I saw a few things in the back cellar. Not much, but it's a start. We can always make a day trip into North Platte."

"I'd love that."

Tom

Tom returned to the bunker with his arms loaded with groceries. He hadn't seen Alex when he came in, so he set down the groceries and went looking for her.

It'd been almost a month since the incident with the Djinn and they had just been spending time together in the depot while her ankle healed.

She had been looking for a job online, but only halfheartedly. She'd also been trying to learn more about hunting. Or at least the lore of what they hunted.

Tom was still adamant she spend as much time sitting as possible.

He found her in the bathroom with a mop and bucket. The whole place smelled like *Pine Sol*.

Tom let out a deep sigh. No matter how much he asked her to stay off her feet, she still did things when he wasn't looking.

"Here you are. What do you think are you doing?" he chided.

She barely spared him a glance. Alex was just wearing leggings and a long shirt. Her feet were bare, and she had tucked her hair under a handkerchief as she cleaned. "I was just trying to pull my weight around here."

"You don't have to do that." He closed the distance to her side.

"Well, someone has to. This place is filthy," she said, returning to her moping.

Tom took the mop from her. "If I can't get you to stay on the couch, at least come help me put the groceries away and we'll decide what to fix for dinner."

Alex let him lead her back to the kitchen, where they started unpacking and putting groceries away.

"I was thinking maybe Chicken Cordon bleu," he said, pulling out a package of raw chicken breast.

She looked at the package, clamped a hand over her mouth, and bolted for the bathroom.

He sighed, pulling a small box out of the bag, and followed her.

Alex was rinsing her mouth out when he appeared in the doorway. "Sorry, I don't know what happened."

Tom held up the box.

She frowned. "Tom, no, I told you I can't—" she started, pain etched on her face.

"Humor me," he said seriously. "There are too many variables that say otherwise."

"What are you talking about?" Her voice still held that very small hint of hope, laced with despair.

"Think about it. You've been nauseous—"

"That was just the pain from my ankle."

"You're exhausted," he continued.

Alex pitched her hands on her hips. "And you've kept me bound to the couch for a month."

"What about you going on this mad cleaning spree?" Tom arched an amused eyebrow. She was cute when she argued.

"Well, have you ever deep cleaned this place?" she deflected.

"What about the fact that the female Djinn was essentially protecting you from her mate consuming you? Maybe she sensed another life."

"Now I think you are really reaching. I'm sorry, Tom. I thought you understood. I'll do this for you. But only if you promise to drop it afterward. And nothing to Gene or Jessica when we head their way next week." Alex snatched the home pregnancy test from his hand, kicked him out, and closed the bathroom door.

Tom looked up at the ceiling hopefully, said a silent prayer, and returned to the kitchen.

His love appeared a few minutes later.

"Well?" he said.

"It takes five minutes."

He set a timer on his phone and started dinner. When the timer went off, he looked at Alex. "Go check." He shooed her toward the bathroom.

She paled and shook her head. Her bottom lip trembled. "I...I can't..."

He wrapped his arms around her, trying to make her feel safe. "No matter what the test says, it will be all right. We have each other. That's what counts. We just need to confirm." He started walking to the bathroom, but she grabbed his arm.

"Please don't be disappointed when it's negative," Alex pleaded, her eyes misty.

"Look, if it's negative, then we continue on as we have been and I'll help you clean the place, but maybe it's positive. Isn't Jade a stone of healing?" he said, bringing up her legal first name that she never used. Tom kissed the top of her head, then he headed down the hall to the bathroom.

**Alex*

Alex was still scared as she watched him walk away. Her heart was beating so hard it made her dizzy. She couldn't bring herself to follow.

She didn't want to see his reaction when the test was negative.

It seemed to take forever for him to return.

When Tom came around the corner into the kitchen, he was staring down at the little white stick.

"Well?" she prodded, both dreading the answer and yet still holding on to that sliver of hope.

He stepped closer and held it out to her.

A little purple plus sign appeared in the window.

Alex blinked.

Could this be true?

Their gazes locked.

Tom's smile widened, and he hugged her, lifting her off the ground and spinning her around.

Tears of joy slid down her cheeks.

She couldn't believe it.

She was going to be a mother.

"How is this possible?" Alex asked when Tom set her back on her feet.

"I know," a woman's voice came from somewhere behind them.

They both spun around.

Alex gasped at the intruder that appeared in the doorway. Although disheveled and bleeding, looking as though she'd taken a severe beating, she was breathtakingly beautiful.

"Neeka, what happened?" Tom asked, as the woman collapsed to the floor. He rushed to her and rolled her over.

She was still conscious, but barely.

"You know her?" Alex asked, still rooted to where she had been.

"Yes, she's the one from the cave. She's Faye. Neeka, who did this to you?" he asked, turning back to the fallen woman.

Alex moved over to them and knelt. "You're the one that helped me save Tom?"

Neeka smiled weakly. "You are named healer, Jade. You just needed some help."

Neeka's eyes fluttered as she passed out. There was a large wound on her lower right side.

"Tom, get me a towel and a first aid kit."

He jumped up and threw a towel at her before going to get the kit. The kit he'd retrieved wasn't a typical first aid kit.

It was a small backpack that Alex had put together after they'd gotten to the depot after the Djinn attack. She worked quickly to stop the bleeding and bandage the Faye woman up.

Tom knelt next to her. "I want to help, but I think I'll just get in the way."

Alex looked up when she'd finished. "We should move her to a bed to rest. Which extra room should we take her to?"

"We have several. But none have been dusted in a while," he said, sheepishly.

"Not the time to worry about that. You get her shoulders, I got her legs," Alex said.

"I feel bad for having you help carry her," Tom said. "I could easily carry her, but it would have required using the fireman's carry to do it, and that could cause the wound to reopen."

They awkwardly carried Neeka to the room a couple of doors down from Tom's and got her settled on the bed.

Alex checked her over, noting her pale lips and clammy skin.

"Will she be okay?" Tom asked.

"She lost a lot of blood. It will take her some time to recover."

"I don't know what could've happened to her," he said, still obviously stunned.

"She looks like she's been in a fight."

"I don't know if Faye engage in fights, but I would've thought she could heal herself."

"She's a what?" Alex asked, frowning.

"A Faye," Tom said. "Fairy Folk. And yes, they are real. Not like Tinkerbell or the like. They can hide among humans without detection. Remember that night in the cave? When I was healed? I told you that your eyes were glowing."

Alex shuddered. "I forgot you said that." She collapsed into the chair, shaking her head.]

"Babe, what's wrong?"

"The Djinn. His eyes were glowing blue. Am I… turning into a Djinn?"

He knelt in front of her. "No, you're not. Your eyes were a warm yellow-white. Like beams of sunlight. It warmed my heart."

"Are you sure?"

"Yes, I'm sure. That night in the cave, I could feel you trying to heal me. When Jessica touched you, Neeka appeared and put a hand on your bestie, and I felt a jolt of power surge into me and mend my wounds."

Alex looked back at Neeka. "There isn't anything more we can do for her tonight. Hopefully, she will rest and wake up in the morning and we can get some fluids down her." She couldn't imagine doing anything else, like what Tom was talking about. Healing him had to be some freak thing, right?

"I don't know what could do this to a Faye, but it's probably something bad. She'd already warned Gene and I that something was coming. And now…now I am going to be a father. I will do whatever it takes to protect you both."

"You think something is coming for me?" Alex blurted, unable to hide the fear inching up from her gut.

"Not you, *per se*. But something is coming. Neeka is proof of that."

Alex led Tom out of the room, turning off the light but leaving the door open a crack.

That night she lay in bed, unable to sleep.

She saw the pregnancy test, but she still didn't believe it.

It can't be real. The doctors said it couldn't happen without help.

She would have to have been on hormones for months before she could've produced an egg capable of being fertilized. It was probably just a false positive.

I can't get my hopes up.

Tom rolled over in his sleep and wrapped his arm around her, his fingers spreading across her belly.

Her heart ached. She wanted to give him children. However, with a half-dead fairy in the other room, was it a good time anyway? Even if the test was right?

Alex let out a sigh and prayed to the night air that things would be all right.

EPILOGUE

*Alex

She ran down the road toward the farmhouse. Her legs were moving too slowly. She had to stop them.

She had to save the baby.

The farmhouse loomed ahead, dark clouds rolling above. She looked at the sky. This was no ordinary storm.

There was evil behind this.

Horrible creatures varying in size from three to seven feet, with wet slimy skin of green and brown that made them more difficult to see, were emerging from the woods.

With each lightning flash, more and more emerged.

They were after Jessica's baby, and she had to stop them.

She ran to the house and up onto the porch.

The door was locked.

"Jess, it's me we gotta go!" Alex screamed.

Behind her, a creature grabbed her and hurled her off the porch.

Three more creatures pounced on her.

She clawed and fought against them, screaming when they pinned her arms and legs to the ground.

. . .

"Alex, Alex!" Tom's voice broke through the dream, and she opened her eyes.

He was kneeling on top of her with one hand holding each of her arms to the bed.

She was panting.

Tom sighed and released his grip and rolled back to his side of the bed.

"What happened?" Alex asked.

He rolled up on an elbow. "You must've been dreaming. You were fighting like a mama bear."

"I was dreaming about Jessica's baby. They were coming to get it," she breathed.

"Who was?" Tom asked.

"Some swamp creatures."

"Like from the horror movie?"

"I don't know. I don't watch scary movies."

"Like covered in moss and dripping water?"

"No, like slimy naked orcs."

"I've heard that pregnancy can cause really odd dreams. Even bad dreams. I'm sure there are more dreams to come. Happy dreams, like this." He gingerly laid a hand across her belly.

Alex curled up on his chest, but what she'd just seen was so much more than just a bad dream.

Was Neeka right?

Could something evil be on the horizon?

ABOUT THE AUTHOR

Andrea Hurtt is an emerging author of various romance categories. She enjoys writing a little bit of everything.

Andrea has been a dental assistant, a stay-at-home mom, owned her own clothing store, was a clothing designer with a vintage-inspired clothing line, Amaryllis Designs, even won Omaha Fashion Week for Top Designer in her category, and Top Boutique for Cancer Survivor Night.

During covid, she wrote four novels, and an award-winning TV pilot screenplay, and moved to Vancouver, BC to pursue acting.

Andrea currently spends her days either writing books or making #EmotionalSupportPillows and traveling around the USA with the cast and fans of the CW TV show Supernatural.

She is the mother of two children, a cat, and a dog, and is a proud Army wife; residing in a haunted Victorian mansion in the Midwest.

Find more information at www.AndreaHurtt.com

ABOUT THE AUTHOR

This is Linda Stecker's second published novel. She enjoys horseback riding, knitting and traveling.
A chance encounter at a community theater audition she didn't even want to attend, Linda and Andrea became quick friends after being thrown on stage together. She has been writing with Andrea Hurtt ever since.

ALSO BY ANDREA HURTT

<u>**Razor's Edge Rockstar Series**</u>

Masquerade - Book One

Undone - Prequel

Unmistakable - Book Two

Incomplete - Book Three

<u>**Love Under Lockdown Series/ Short Stories**</u>

Acting The Part

Truth or Dare

<u>**Demons Within Us Series**</u>

Nebraska Nights

Depot Dreams

COMING SOON

<u>**Heartthrob Collective Series**</u>

*Batteries Not Required

My Night with Sonic Vibe

<u>**Razor's Edge Rockstar Romance Series**</u>

Drowning - Book Four

Inconsolable - Book Five

AVAILABLE ON AMAZON AND ANDREAHURTT.COM